Beyond the Tangled Mountain

Beyond the Tangled Mountain

by
DOUGLAS C. PERCY

A Sequel to "Hidden Valley"
and "When the Bamboo Sings"

HORIZON BOOKS
Box 600
Beaverlodge, Alberta, Canada

BEYOND THE TANGLED MOUNTAIN

DEDICATED

with a sense of complete inadequacy and humility

to

Mabel Brown and Peggy Maxson

Copyright 1962 by
Zondervan Publishing House
Grand Rapids, Michigan

Assigned 1975 to
Horizon House Publishers
All Rights Reserved

ISBN 0-88965-002-0

HORIZON BOOKS
are published by Horizon House Publishers
Box 600, Beaverlodge, Alberta, Canada T0H 0C0
Printed in the United States of America

In this book you will meet again the characters of *Hidden Valley* and *When the Bamboo Sings,* with the addition of some others whom I trust you will accept into our circle. And once again I should mention the fact that this story has its counterpart in real life, with some of the circumstances and locations changed.

The story grew out of the experiences of two dear friends for whom I have the utmost admiration and respect. To them I have dedicated this book, for they both faced a tangled mountain of pain, doubt, and despair.

One of them, a graduate nurse, had dedicated her life for missionary service in Africa. During her first year at a Bible institute, she fell prey to polio, and all the dreams and plans toppled. And so, almost, did she. Then in one of those sublime moments she had an experience with God, and she surrendered her partially paralyzed body for whatever the Lord would have her to do. As I heard the story, it went something like this: In the rehabilitation center, attempts were made to restore the use of arms and legs. Then one day, the doctor spoke of a concentrated effort, saying that if they worked on hands *or* legs, there was more likelihood of success in some degree. In the simplicity of faith that staggers one, this friend said in effect: "With my hands I may yet serve the Lord. Give me the use of my hands."

Today she is confined to a wheel chair, but those hands are full and blessed. She returned to University, attained a nursing science degree, and is now engaged by a large hospital in Canada, helping to train other nurses, doubtless praying in her heart that many might go in her place to the dark continent. She teaches Sunday school, sings, speaks, and above all lives one of those fragrant lives that God seems to bring out of the depths of suffering.

The other to whom this book is dedicated has a somewhat different story. She was a missionary in Aden, Arabia, doubtless one of the hottest places on the face of the earth. And there she served, until in one blinding, blasting stroke she found herself in an antiquated iron lung, paralyzed from chin to ankles. The story of her heroism and spiritual power might take a book in itself. The slow recovery from the clutch of death; the agonizing realization of helplessness; the birth of a baby while still paralyzed, and the return home to a life of uselessness — this seemed to be her course. Uselessness? No, the story follows a vastly different path. There was the grim determination to gain the use, at least partially, of a wasted, helpless body. There were prayer and faith and courage. There was the use of a four-wheeled stroller, and the agony of thinking muscles into action. Then months and months later the halting, limping walk with crutches. Then the transition to canes . . . . and soon the miracle of walking with only a slight limp.

And now? With a courage that staggers one, she returned to Aden with her family to take up again, with an increased sense of the calling and the enabling of God, the work that *must* be accomplished — reaching the unreached for Christ.

Our story fails to set all this forth. But if in a small measure the reader will realize a new triumph in Christ and be ready to glorify Him whether by life or by death, then you will know the theme of our book, that it is gloriously possible to go

BEYOND THE TANGLED MOUNTAIN.

Douglas C. Percy

Toronto, Ontario

One

The sea laughed.

It thrilled beneath the warm light breath of the wind, its surface covered with faint ripples, dazzlingly reflecting the sun like a thousand silver lips laughing back to the sky. It laughed too at the great white and gold ship that cleft its smooth waters, rolling back the foamy edges like finest lace.

Then the laughter burst forth in a long, loud peal of pure joy as, poised as high on the bow of the ship as she could get, Jane McAdams flung her arms up, the wind pressing closely about her, streaming her hair and carrying her voice back along the deck.

At the top of the gangway leading down to her level stood Dr. Bill McAdams, dark of hair and darkly bronzed by this tropical sun. His hands rested lightly on the rail to steady himself against the faint roll of the Nigeria-bound *Abosso*, as with appreciative eye he watched the small, slim figure of his wife at the bow. Then as his ear caught the sound of her laughter, he gripped the rails of the steep stairway, leaned forward and, giving himself a slight push with his feet, slid noiselessly on his hands down to the lower deck. A series of short jumps helped him to recover his balance, and then on tip-toe he approached the girl.

Suddenly his long arms shot out, binding her upstretched arms, then quickly his hands covered her eyes.

A squeal and a twist only brought her closer into his arms, then teasingly he uncovered her eyes. As she turned to see who it was, he impulsively bent and kissed her laughing mouth.

"Bill," the girl gasped the one word, then fell to giggling and laughing again.

"What's so funny?" the man asked. "I heard you laughing all the way back to the stern. I think the captain is coming to see what the noise is all about."

7

"Oh, he *isn't!*" Then, realizing her husband's joke, she went on, "Have you ever heard or seen a porpoise laugh?"

"Well, if you're a porpoise I have," remarked Bill. "But what's the joke?"

"Come here," and catching his thumb in a familiar gesture, she pulled him to the rail. "Look down there," and she pointed immediately in front of the prow, cutting like a knife through the rippled water.

He looked. The giant pear-shaped porpoises were lazily arching across the prow of the fast approaching boat. As they rose effortlessly from the water, shining and sleek, they seemed to turn their pointed faces to the boat, opened their mouths in a great thick-lipped, toothy grin, then disappeared under the surface just as the boat reached them. This could only be the laughter that his wife had mentioned. Bill McAdams chuckled, then as he watched he suddenly heard himself laughing out loud at these clowns of the sea doing their comic turn.

"Shhhh . . ." he felt a hand on his arm and turned to see his wife with her finger to her lips. He looked quizzically, then as he followed her sweeping hand, he heard her say: "Shhhh. . . . the captain will hear you."

With another laugh she bounded away, racing along the deck and up the stairway like a gazelle, with Bill bounding after her. He caught her as she reached the top of the stairs, where panting and laughing at the same time, she stopped her headlong pace and began to move slowly along the deck.

They walked in silence for a few minutes, then as they reached the end of the deck walk, they moved to the reclining chairs in the shade and sat down.

"Another two days," said Bill, "and we dock at Apapa wharf. We'll stop just long enough to clear our gear and station wagon through customs, then head inland and home . . ." and he squeezed the hand that was snuggled into his great fist.

"Home," she repeated dreamily, "home . . . it's where the heart is. Bill," she turned to him, suddenly quiet, "do you think I'll make a good missionary? I seem to have so little of what it takes. All I can really do is play the piano, and I won't even have that to work on for the next four years."

Bill did not answer immediately. The sun had begun to fall, and on the tropical waters it falls quickly. The world holds its breath for a moment. The heart quickens as the waters ignite, then almost breathlessly the fiery color extinguishes itself, softly slipping the world at sea into gentle darkness.

In the now dim light, he turned to his wife. "Jane dear," he spoke quietly, befitting the mood of the early evening, "you have given your life to Christ. That is all that He wants. He will make you the missionary He wants you to be. . . . You can't be trained for it except in a spiritual sense. When you have learned some of the language, learned the needs of the people, and feel for them in those needs . . . you will find yourself a missionary — a sent one."

They were both quiet awhile. Then he went on. "I'll be anxious to get word from Peter Dunning about the possibility of a nurse coming out to help us. With competent help, I should be able to get away more and into the back country where I first met Chuna. My, it will be good to see the rascal again. And Baru too. . . ." and his voice trailed away in a flood of memories.

Baru and Dr. McAdams had been on trek when he had been able to rescue Chuna from the beating with bamboo rods that was to prove his manhood and make him acceptable as the husband of Salamatu, the daughter of the witch doctor Tamanta. From that amazing adventure had come the opening of missionary work among the fierce Kitta people and the conversion of the old witch doctor himself.*

As he thought of those days of adventure, his heart ached for the sight of the Africans whom he had grown to love so much, and a deep sigh echoed across the deck.

"A penny. . . ." whispered a voice beside him, and suddenly he realized that from now on he would be sharing those days and friends with his partner. He reached over and pulled her head onto his shoulder, then almost dreamily he began to talk:

"Jane," he was speaking very quietly, "married life in Africa is not like life at home. I will have work and more work all the time. You won't be seeing me then as much as you are now. . . ."

". . . but I have you in my heart," she interrupted him, "and we have both surrendered one another to Christ. I'll be content," and she settled her head back on his shoulder.

"Then let me tell you about my dream, which I hope to start realizing as soon as we get settled," he said. "Down near the great valley where Chuna found Salamatu, there is a mountain range that cuts right across the foot of the valley. The Africans have told me that there are many, many villages there that no one seems to know about. One of my first jobs after we get the hospital rolling again will be to go out and look it over.

* Told in *When the Bamboo Sings* by the same author.

"It's funny," he went on, "but the Africans have two names for it. One is Bima, which they say is a name that Mohammed gave it when he rode his camel across the end of the valley. It means judgment, and according to tradition, a man can be judged at the mountain."

"How?" asked Jane, all curious about this new country that so soon was to be her home.

"Well, it seems that Mohammed's camel stepped on some soft rock and left two large prints behind, a camel's stride apart. The story goes on to say that if a righteous man blows into one hole, water will spout up from the other. If he is unrighteous, nothing happens," and McAdams chuckled. "I don't think I'll risk taking chances — not with anyone watching anyway."

"Oh, I'm sure it would be a veritable Niagara," murmured Jane, then ducked to dodge the hand that shot out at her.

"What's the other name for the mountain?" she asked after a moment or two.

"I've been trying to think of it," replied her husband. "I know it in Hausa all right, but I don't know how to translate it. Evidently the mountain is a series of tremendous boulders scattered every which way, as though some giant had knocked over a set of great blocks. These rocks are overgrown with a strong thorn bush, making most of the way across impassable. I think the best way to interpret it is 'The Tangled Mountain.' But that doesn't sound very romantic, so I always call it Bima, and then tell how man can be judged by it."

He continued to talk, opening up to his wife more and more of the lore he had absorbed during his years as the medical missionary in that far-flung northeast section of Nigeria.

Suddenly the dinner bell pealed through the ship, and Bill took his wife's hand, drew her to her feet, then with his hand under her elbow guided her towards the softly lighted dining room.

Just before stepping inside, they both turned and looked out at the black of the night, only faintly illuminated by the stars that dipped and twinkled overhead. They waited a moment in silence, listening to the soft gurgle of water pealed back by the sharp-prowed ship.

"They are still laughing," said Bill. Then together they went down for dinner.

Two

The quiet of the ship's lounge was broken by a booming voice, and both Jane and Bill jerked around to meet its owner. To Bill it seemed as though they met head-on, the owner of the deep voice. It was almost a physical encounter.

"There you are, dearie!" The large body fitted the boom of the voice exactly. "We've been looking all over for you since before dinner."

Both the McAdamses rose to their feet. "We were out on the prow watching the porpoise play, Mrs. Wigle" (*"Wiggle" as Bill calls her,* thought Jane irreverently).

"Well, my husband and I did so want to talk to Dr. Mc-Adams about that there Africa." Everything in her vocabulary was punctuated with "that there." "So we decided that we could sit down and have a nice talk." And suiting action to her words, she sat down on a settee for two, leaving room for none, and looked around. Bill and Jane followed her gaze and saw, standing at the lounge doorway, the meek and mild Mr. Wigle.

"Over here, dear," the command from his wife was like a whistle, and with dog-like docility he shuffled over, looked askance at the remainder of the settee so fully occupied by his wife, then pulled a chair over.

"Yes, Dr. McAdams" — his voice, belying his size, was deep, with a peculiar and fascinating resonance — "we will be landing in a day or so, and I wondered if you could give us some hints as to where to go and what we should do."

The booming voice of his wife cut across, somewhat like a foghorn interrupting a symphony: "And do you know any of the people we could meet in Lagos? And what should we do about that there malaria we hear so much about. Personally I find that them there 'aspirine' tablets are enough to knock any little fever out of me."

Aspirin, thought Bill. Then he remembered his friend

11

Peter Dunning, whose medical knowledge consisted of "aspirin above the neck, epsom salts below, and iodine on the outside." His memory forced a laugh that he immediately checked as he found the eyes of the woman on him questioningly. He began to feel overwhelmed with presence and words, but the end was not yet.

"You know, my dear," she had turned to the doctor's wife, "this is our first trip away from home. And why Merle picked Africa," (she turned her large eyes on that hapless man. The two young people couldn't imagine him picking anything but a wife, and that only in the way an apple picks a farmer!) "I'll never know. But here we are, and we're going to enjoy it. Aren't we, Merle?" Then without waiting for an answer, or perhaps not expecting one, she turned back to Jane.

"As I was saying," there was no break in her voice, jumping from topic to topic, "this is our first trip away from home. Ten years ago, Merle picked up some stock, and then forgot about it. Then one day he was asked when he was going to clip and cash his coupons" (she pronounced it *cowpoons*) "and when we went down to see what it was all about we found it was worth $50,000. So here we are, and them there stocks were good after all." As she looked for a moment at her spouse, Bill could realize the recrimination that had been his for the impulsive buying. Now all was well. Bill saw a secret smile at the corners of the man's mouth. *I'd like to talk to him alone,* thought Bill. *He looks as though he has a man hidden under that meek and mild exterior. As for his wife, she doesn't know much, but she knows it fluently.* He turned back to the two women.

"Perhaps Bill can help you," Jane had managed to break into the spate of words that tumbled over each other. "I've never been to Africa before either, so I'll be learning too."

The woman turned to Bill. "I'll be glad to help you, Mrs. Wigle," he caught himself just in time, the "Wiggle" bitten off on his tongue. "And I do have some friends in Lagos who will be glad to show you around. What you should get is a reliable African man who will serve as a guide for you. I'll see what can be done when we arrive.

"As for malaria, it's a real threat, all right. And I'm afraid that aspirin won't help too much. There are several prophylactics that you can get, and if you take one faithfully, you shouldn't have too much trouble. Quinine is basic, of course, but the other preparations that have been developed are excellent, too, and don't have to be taken so regularly. I'll give you a list, and you can get them at the Kingsway store as soon as we arrive."

"Store?" The question rocketed from the settee. "Stores in Africa? You mean a witch doctor's hut, I suppose?" and the voice expressed complete disbelief.

Bill did laugh this time. "You are going to be surprised," he said at last. "Africa is more modern than tomorrow and more primitive than the stone age. You can travel a dozen miles and be a thousand years apart in the culture and life of the people. The Kingsway store I mentioned is part of the giant United Africa Company. It has a supermarket, as you call it, in Lagos. And I've seen other stores with just a grass roof in some out-of-the-way village. But you have to see Africa to believe it. It will be worth every one of your 'cowpoons,'" he couldn't resist it, though he heard Jane's sibilant *"Bill"* beside him.

The woman missed the mimicry. "Do tell," she exclaimed. "Hear that, Merle? Africa is civilized." The quiet Merle merely nodded his head.

"You will look after us in Lagos then?" she turned to Bill, who was convinced that he was the first man to whom she had ever appealed for help. And he knew that only the strangeness of their surroundings and the uncertainty of the new country brought her to such a condition.

"Be glad to," he replied, mentally reviewing some of the surprises that he would have in store for them. "And I'll keep you from ending up in a cannibal's pot," and again he laughed as he saw her stiffen.

"Bill is joking of course, Mrs. Wigle," said Jane, the eternal feminine, coming to the rescue of her sex, "but he has seen and lived through some experiences that make me realize that there is still a lot that is dark and foreboding in this country."

"Really?" and the woman turned back to Bill. "You know I thought that you missionaries just stood under·a palm tree with a Bible in your hands, while adoring Africans stood around and listened to you. . . ."

". . . and then burnt their idols and put on mother hubbards and lived perfectly useless lives ever after," Bill interrupted her to say. "Well, I guess that is what a lot of people believe. Tell you what," he leaned forward. "I will invite you and your husband to visit us as soon as we can get the mission house in order. Will you come?"

"We will," the voice behind the woman almost made the

three of them jump. It was Mr. Wigle, who hadn't moved, and it seemed as though he hadn't spoken. But it was his voice with its ringing timbre, and even his wife didn't argue with him this time.

"We'd love it," she replied, putting a large hand on Jane's arm. "Just think, seeing a missionary doctor at work. . . ." and her voice trailed off.

Bill wanted to turn the conversation. "Jane" — she turned to her husband — "in a few days you will say good-by to pianos for four years. How about storing up some memories on that beautiful Baldwin grand over there," and he waved to the other side of the lounge.

"Oh, do you play?" enquired Mrs. Wigle, in the voice used for the children of friends who insist on them playing for company. "I'd love to hear you."

Without a word, Jane got up and moved with her own peculiar gazelle-like grace, toes slightly in, to the piano. Raising the top and setting it on its arm, she opened the keyboard, then sat down and rippled through some chords to limber up her fingers. Then quietly she began the opening bars of Beethoven's *Appassionata Sonata*. Soon oblivious to everything but the music, her body slightly bent forward, her lower lip sucked in in its characteristic position, she played on.

Bill heard a rustle and looked around. As though there had been an announcement, people began to drift into the lounge, quietly and unobtrusively seating themselves, drawn by the superb music.

The sonata finished, she bridged with a few chords, then began the hauntingly beautiful *Moonlight Sonata*. Time seemed to stand still, even the motion of the boat seemed poised as the girl played on and on, the great classics performed with the flawless technique and deep passion of the master musician.

Then from nowhere and from everywhere came a peculiar change in the phrasing. The fingers seemed to be caressing the keys, and from the stringed depths of the Baldwin came the simple refrain of "Day Is Dying in the West." And with the repeated, "Holy, Holy, Holy, Lord God Almighty," Bill saw several people look at each other in surprise, then settle back as familiar words linked themselves to the music.

Idly, Bill looked around. A man was stealthily knocking the ashes from a cigar, then extinguishing it in the ashes. One woman, whose poise and posturing had been the center of attention during the whole voyage, seemed to be dropping back into reality, and sat transfixed as the music rolled over and over her.

"What a Friend We Have in Jesus. . . ." Bill subconsciously heard the words, and saw several people moving their mouths as though keeping up with the music as childhood memories supplied the words. "I've Found a Friend, Oh, Such a Friend," the link in Jane's mind was transmitted to her fingers and, still oblivious to her audience, she played on.

Once again Bill's eyes were on Jane. He saw her suck in her lips, then heard her play as she had the first time he had met her, and his eyes misted with the memory. 'Her fingers were moving gently, as though feeling for something to express a mood that had gathered upon her. Out of the first flurry of the keys came a light, tinkling harmony. It tickled the ear for a moment, then was gone, only to return again in the midst of a cascade of notes.

And each time, lost then found, the tune returned, clearer and sharper than before. Then the mind registered the words:

From Greenland's icy mountains, from India's coral strand,
Where Afric's sunny fountains roll down their golden
    sand. . . .

The movement was from minor to major, a rhythmic roll of music that carried the refrain without letting it get lost even once. It seemed as though there was whispered in the room the words . . .

From many an ancient river . . .

And the rippling of the water could be heard as her right hand trilled with amazing technique in the upper register.

From many a palmy plain . . .

There was a musical rustle, like a breeze riffling the stiff palm fronds,

They call us to deliver . . .

And the instrument spoke. With some musical magic, those flying fingers produced a medley of voices, shrill, staccato, deep and bass, that were plaintive in vain repetition.

The people seemed to jump. From nowhere had come a crash, a great symphony of raging chords that was being hurled out of the piano:

They call us to deliver
Their land from error's chain.

The silence after the crash could almost be heard. Then, tinkling clear, sometimes in single notes, pure and crystal clear, bringing again the words:

Shall we, whose souls are lighted,
With wisdom from on high,
Shall we to men benighted,
The lamp of life deny?

Then as Bill so well remembered, there came the question, repeated over and over again with perfect phrasing: *Shall we? Shall we? Shall we?*

Then dancing lightly over the keyboard that almost made the words to burst forth in a paean of praise:

Salvation, oh salvation,
That joyful sound proclaim,
Till every tribe and nation
Has heard of Jesus' Name.

The music slowed, and almost with a sigh Bill relaxed the pressure of his clasped hands.

And as he did, he heard the simple Bach choral, "Jesu, Joy of Man's Desiring." Over and over, in every variation as set down by the immortal composer, "Jesu, joy of man's desiring" rang out through the lounge.

And still the people sat, transfixed by this amazing arrangement of classical and sacred music that spoke more than a hundred sermons.

Jane was on the last run. Her lower lip was relaxed, and she smiled. Then for the first time, she looked up toward Bill. Her range of vision swept around the lounge and she saw the people. Her eyes started, and only her trained and disciplined artistry kept her fingers on the keyboard. But as the piece finished, her face suffused with a blush that enveloped her neck and head.

There was an awed silence for a moment. Then spontaneously, and almost worshipfully, the people clapped. It was no music hall applause. It was the expression of people moved and moved deeply. And as the clapping died away Bill felt a hand on his arm.

Mrs. Wigle, her huge hand biting deeply into his forearm, her eyes moist in her great round face, for once was speechless. A soundless "thank you, thank you" was seen in the shaped lips, then she rose and walked quickly out of the lounge.

Slowly the people came to Jane, a "thank you" here, a hand shake there, then they too left, perhaps to think of what they had heard.

Bill and Jane were alone. Or almost alone. As the last of

the people left, a figure rose out of a chair in the shadows. It was Mr. Wigle.

Diffidently he came forward. Alone, he did not seem to be so small nor insignificant. It was his wife's overpowering voice and great size that made the contrast. Now Bill saw a man of medium height, a fine looking man in a rough-hewn way, iron gray hair parted carefully but showing its tendency to be unruly.

"Dr. McAdams," Bill was again amazed at the voice, "and Mrs. McAdams," he turned to Jane still seated at the piano, "I just want to thank you for one of the most wonderful evenings I have ever known." He paused, as though unused to making speeches, and indeed seemed to look around to have his wife interrupt and finish his sentence. "I've been wanting to talk to you ever since I heard there was a missionary on board." Again he stopped. "Perhaps you have wondered why my wife and I are heading for Africa." He looked at the two quizzically, a shade of a smile on his face. "Yes, it was my idea," he said, as though answering an unspoken question, "although I think my wife would at least like half the credit," and his fine eyes twinkled.

Bill warmed to the man, but said nothing to interrupt. Jane got up from the piano to join them as they stood in the center of the lounge.

"How long have you been a missionary?" he asked abruptly.

"I spent four years in Nigeria," replied Bill. "My wife is going out for the first time."

"Did you always want to be a missionary?" again the question was almost peremptory.

"Far from it," replied Bill honestly. "I had other ideas about my life. That is until I paid a visit out here to my friend Peter Dunning. Then I knew it was the only life for me."

Mr. Wigle was silent for a moment. Then, "You'll forgive me, Dr. McAdams, but I just feel I want to talk to someone." He paused. "When I was a young man I had a peculiar experience." Again he paused, as though doubtful about what to say next. Then almost shrugging, he continued: "I was attending a special evangelistic service with the rest of our young people's society. I went along for the ride — the buggy ride, I might say," he added with a grin that completely transformed his face. "We had to ride 12 miles, and anything would do to get us off the farm for a couple of hours.

"That night for the first time I heard why Christ had come into the world, why He had died, and what His resurrection meant. A bunch of us went forward — 'hitting the sawdust trail,' we were told — but whatever it was I believed on the Lord Jesus Christ and was saved." His chin lifted a little as though expecting ridicule. When Bill only nodded sympathetically, he went on:

"The man who was the evangelist spoke to each one of us, suggesting some of the things that we should do now that we were Christians. Then he added, and I'll never forget the exact words: 'You have taken the greatest step of your life, but it is not the last. From now on you belong to the Lord Jesus Christ and must seek to honor and to serve Him wherever you are and whatever you do.'" The beautifully modulated voice almost dropped to a whisper. "And from that time on I felt I had to be a missionary. I felt 'called,' if you like, and seemed to think of nothing else.

"Then Alma came along." He smiled. "That's my wife. Will you believe it when I say that she was the most lithesome and beautiful girl in our whole valley?" He smiled at the memory. "And believe it or not, dear friends, I think she still is . . . inside. Our hard farm life and four children put on the weight you see and made her more of a man than some men. But I assure you she is a woman inside." He said it simply.

"But I'm ahead of myself," he closed his eyes for a moment. "When I saw Alma, I forgot about being a missionary or anything else. I just wanted to give her everything she deserved. I went to agricultural college, specialized in breeding and raising chickens, and developed a special strain that gave me a continent-wide market. But in developing that good strain, my spiritual life went undeveloped. I forgot everything but my work and my family.

"Then a few years ago I heard about those five young men being killed in South America while seeking to enter the wild Auca territory. In quick succession it seemed as though the whole world turned topsy turvy: the Far East, the Middle East, South America, Africa . . . and I asked myself if I had forgotten myself a little more and remembered God and others a little more, if things might have been different. So now," he looked at them both, almost imperiously, "I'm going to be a missionary and raise chickens to pay expenses," and he almost chuckled as he said it.

All this while they had been standing, but when he finished they moved to a large sectional seat and sat down. They were all silent for a moment.

Breaking the silence, Jane said: "Mr. Wigle, you are looking at another one who was just like you. I'm only grateful that I did not remain as hard as I tried to be, and that I am now on my way to serve where He wants me to serve."

Bill felt a little strange talking to this man almost twenty-five years his senior. Yet he felt he should. "Mr. Wigle," he began, "I think that there are many people who miss God's best, but it is never too late when you do wake up. And I am sure that you will find something to do yet — even in Africa."

"Tell you what," replied the other man, "I'm not really interested in sightseeing, though for Alma's sake I think we should do some. But as soon as we can we will come to your station, and perhaps really talk out this work that I really want to do."

"It's a deal," said Bill, putting out his hand. It was taken firmly and clasped for a moment, then with a flip of the hand to Jane, Mr. Wigle left.

Jane turned to Bill, her eyes brimming with emotion. "Why didn't you signal me that all those people were coming in to listen?" she demanded.

Bill wrinkled up his nose at her. "Because," he replied, man-like, "I was enjoying it too much. And I was enjoying their enjoyment of it too," he went on proudly. "After all, they don't have wives who can play like Jubal Cain who made the listening angels 'standing round, fall at hearing such celestial sound,'" and he struck a pose as he declaimed his two lines of poetry.

Jane swung her little fist at him, and it was immediately imprisoned in his own. "Look, Mrs. McAdams," he drew her closer to him, "I won't be able to hear you play for four years, and I want to get all I can in the meantime. So when I give a command performance . . . PLAY!" and he swung his free arm imperiously.

"Look, Mr. Man," and suddenly she knew the name would be his from then on, "I'll play for you only whenever I want to — which is all the time," she added hurriedly. Then pulling her hand free, she slipped outside.

Three

Outside of the lounge, the darkness of the night seemed more intense, and Jane paused for a moment for her eyes to adjust to the change in light. After a moment she moved slowly across the deck to the rail. And as she did so, a large figure loomed out of the shadows.

"Mrs. McAdams?" The voice startled her. But with her eyes now used to the darkness, she made out the large face and the bright eyes of Mrs. Wigle. "I've been waiting to talk to you and to thank you for that there music we had tonight." Out on the deck and with the evening breeze carrying the voice along, it did not seem as shrill or strident as in the confines of the lounge.

She went on before Jane had an opportunity to say anything: "I didn't dare wait in there to speak to you, so I waited out here. I watched Merle speaking to you," she went on, "and I don't know what he said. He is such a quiet one," and Jane smiled at the recollection of the conversation.

"Can I talk to you somewhere," she went on, speaking close to Jane's ear. "There is something I would like to say." Without waiting for further reply, she took Jane's arm and led her to where the deck chairs were chained to a bar to prevent their sliding to the rail if the ship should roll. They sat down and were silent for a few minutes. Then with a sigh, Mrs. Wigle began to speak.

"I don't know why I tell you this," she said, speaking hesitantly, "but as soon as I heard that there were missionaries on board, I wanted to talk to you. I was glad of the chance tonight, in that there lounge, but I didn't say the right things." Again she paused.

"You know," she went on, "Merle is just so keen to see different countries, that I even let him pick our first trip to Africa. But if I had chosen it, I would have picked Africa too. May I tell you why?" For her, she was almost humble.

When Jane nodded, the woman went on: "When I was a young girl," and she laughed shyly as she turned her face to Jane, "I really was, once—and I think I was some looker too," almost coarsely the expression came out. "Anyway, I was proud of my looks and my figure, and mostly because I had my eye on Merle. You should hear him sing," she exclaimed suddenly. "I doubt if the angels will please me as much." Again she gave what was almost a giggle that shook her vast frame, then was serious. "When we were young people, a revival came to our valley, and one night when none of my close friends were around, I went forward to accept Christ as my Saviour. Then when I got home I thought of all that I would have to give up if I went on with it, and decided then and there that there would be no more religion for me than I needed to keep up with everyone else in that there valley. Just before I went to sleep that night, just as clearly as I heard you play that there music, I heard a voice saying: 'Alma, you must be a missionary. You must be a missionary.' And I can still hear myself saying as I buried my ears in the pillow: 'No, No, No!' And from then on, although nobody ever knew it, I was cold inside.

"I saw that Merle liked me, and I made it easy for him to win me. Hah!" she almost snorted, "win me! I won him, and I'm glad I did. He has been a good man, and that there stock he bought when I didn't want him to waste his money was just one of the many wise things he did. He's the best hatchery man in the country, if I do say so," and she was proud.

"I never did tell Merle about my experience, nor the missionary bit, and I suppose he will never know. But as soon as we were financially free and Merle talked about traveling, I felt that this might be another chance for me. I suppose that we will have to do a lot of sightseeing, since that is what he wants, but I am more interested in missionary work. Do you think, if I induce Merle, that we could spend a little time with you on your station?"

Jane sat stunned. Almost the same story, the same words, the same longing. She sat so long and so silently that Mrs. Wigle felt she had gone too far.

"I'm sorry to have bothered you," she began somewhat stiffly, her whole tone changed.

Jane put out a hand. "Dear Mrs. Wigle, you don't need to feel that I am not interested. What you have just said, I have heard before, and indeed it was almost my own story. May I talk to you about it tomorrow?" she asked impulsively, a dazzling idea coming to her.

"Yes, dearie," said the older woman, "that there music must have tired you out. You get some rest, and I'll see you tomorrow."

"It isn't quite that," went on Jane slowly, feeling her way. This counseling was new to her and she hesitated at saying the wrong thing. "I was just thinking how much Bill and I think as one and work as one, even though we have been married such a short time. Mrs. Wigle," the words came easier now, "why don't you go and have a talk with your husband. Tell him what you have just told me. He may be more interested in this than you think."

"Not Merle," chuckled the woman. "Anything that doesn't cackle or lay eggs has no interest for him. That and seeing new sights," she added.

"Try it anyway," insisted Jane. "It is much more fun and wonderful to want to do things together. You've both lived such busy lives that you haven't taken time to talk about what to do with this free time you have. *Do* try it," and she laid an appealing hand on the woman's arm.

"All right, I will," replied Mrs. Wigle after a time, "but he won't understand, particularly about me going forward that night in that there meeting."

The two got up, then almost impulsively Jane leaned forward and kissed Mrs. Wigle on the cheek. "Good night, dear friend," she said, "I'll be praying for you tonight."

Then they moved silently to the stairway and down to their cabins. In Jane's heart was a strange warmth and sense of complete peace. What a surprise the Wigles would have in their cabin that night. Jane ran the last few feet to her cabin. She wanted to tell Bill.

Four

The next morning, Bill and Jane were sitting at breakfast when the Wigles entered the dining room. The two had been waiting, toying with their food, hoping that the couple would put in an appearance. The McAdamses were completely unprepared for what they saw.

The entrance of Mrs. Wigle into the dining room or any other part of the ship had invariably given a sense of overpowering physical presence. Loud of voice, strident in tone, heavy of foot, she had become the cynosure of all eyes whenever she put in an appearance. And the invariable following of Mr. Wigle gave the impression of a pet poodle at the heels of a stern mistress.

This morning it was different. If the young missionaries had not been looking for them, the Wigles might have slipped into the dining room unnoticed. As it was, they were half way across the floor before they were seen. Mrs. Wigle was walking, lightly one would almost say, her arm through that of her husband. And he, with head high and shoulders back, seemed a man for the first time on the long voyage. The two of them had such looks on their face that Bill nudged Jane.

"They look like bride and groom," he whispered behind the menu that he raised to hide the motion of his lips, all the while his eyes on the couple. Then raising the menu, he waved it slightly to get the attention of the older couple, who immediately changed their course and moved over to their table.

Mrs. Wigle reached them first. Standing behind Jane's chair, she put a hand on the girl's shoulder and said, so softly that she had to strain her hearing to get it all:

"You knew all the time, dearie?" and even the endearment was no longer cheap and shallow. It had a new quality, coming as it did so unexpectedly from this massive woman. As Jane nodded her head, the woman went on: "I talked to Merle as you suggested last night, and before I was through we were both crying like a couple of children," and she sent a beaming smile over to her husband who was chatting quietly with Bill.

Then she went on: "I don't think I was ever so nervous nor so completely surprised as I was by that there talk we had. And you know, Mrs. — may I call you Jane, Mrs. McAdams?" and at the latter's quick, "Oh do," she continued, "and you know, Jane, it seemed as though for the first time that Merle and I really understood each other." She giggled, which in her meant a convulsive heave. "And I actually felt married for the first time in years," and she smiled a crooked smile at the girl who was looking up at her with beaming face and tear-dimmed eyes.

"Dear Mrs. Wigle," Jane put her hand up and covered the one resting lightly on her shoulder, "I felt last night that you must tell your husband. But do sit down here," she said impulsively. "I'm sure the stewards won't mind you changing your table for one meal."

No more invitation was needed. Mr. Wigle was already sitting, talking earnestly and quietly to Bill, and his wife quickly pulled out the other chair at the table and sat down.

As the steward sidled up to get their order, the conversation was broken for a moment, but as soon as he was gone, Mr. Wigle turned to Jane.

"I understand that I have you to thank for this very sudden and unexpected turn of events," and his voice and eyes were warm with emotion. "I don't know when I have been more surprised than when Alma came into the cabin in tears last night, and then told me what she had told you," and he stretched his hand out across the table to have it grasped by his wife. "Now we have a lot to talk about and time to make up. What a fool I have been," and his eyes clouded.

"No, Merle" — this new, subdued voice was something that Jane was finding hard to adjust to — "I have been the fool. And worse," and Mrs. Wigle dabbed at her eyes with her free hand. "But we can make it up, Merle, and I want you to tell these here people what we talked about last night." Her change seemed complete. For the first time on the voyage, Jane heard her turn to her husband and give him the opportunity to speak and to lead. It seemed the final submission.

Merle Wigle evidently felt so too, for he just sat for the longest moment looking into the eyes of his wife. Perhaps he was seeing once again, the slim, lithe girl he had met and married thirty-five years before. And he was seeing a new woman. The flicker in his eye and the new note in his voice spoke of it.

"Alma and I feel that we both have a great deal to make up for," he began, speaking quietly. Then he stopped as the steward placed their breakfast before them. When they were alone again, he continued: "We may not have much time or skill to offer, but we do have some money, which we want to use wisely and fully. Dr. McAdams — " he was interrupted by the missionary, "It's Bill."

"Bill then," the older man picked up the threads of his conversation, "I'm going to depend on you for some advice and counsel for these next few months that we will have in Africa." He picked up a spoon and began to eat his cereal. He ate in silence for awhile, then put the spoon down. "Don't get me wrong," and he smiled his slow smile, "I'm not trying to pay off or buy out any obligation or shortcoming. I couldn't sleep last night, and have been going over and over in my mind what to do. Then when I was sure Alma was asleep, I got out of bed. . . ."

"I saw you," interrupted his wife, a lifelong habit exerting itself. Then catching herself up, she blushed a little, and then more quietly said, "I couldn't sleep either, and I saw you get up and kneel down to pray. So I stayed in bed, but I prayed with you," and she sent a smile over to her husband that transformed the large, round face. He smiled back, then went on:

"Well, we both prayed then, and that makes it all the more unanimous," and he chuckled. "I prayed, really prayed, for the first time in many years. Some of that prayer is too personal to talk about. But things came to my mind in answer to my praying.

"There are two things I want to ask you, and I want frank and candid answers," and he waggled a finger at Bill. "The first thing is, we want to show our appreciation for what you have done for us in the past twelve hours, and we want to get something for your mission hospital that you need desperately. The other — well, you answer the one first, and I'll tell you what the second thing is."

Bill was embarrassed. "Really," he almost stammered, "we didn't do anything for you. The Lord spoke to you, and the credit and the glory are His."

Wigle waved his hand. "Young man, you are not telling me anything I don't already know. The Lord used you, or rather your wife's playing last night to get through to us," and he sent a smile of appreciation in Jane's direction, "and we have thanked Him for it, and will continue to do so. But I also felt when I was praying that I have money that must be used to the best advantage now, and since your work is the first that I have heard about I want to do something to help it along. I may not be saying it right, but I think you understand what I mean," and he looked almost pleadingly at Bill.

The doctor succumbed to the appeal of the look. "I do understand," he said. "I just want you to know that it is not for us nor to us but to the Lord, if you give anything." The other man nodded.

"Then I'll tell you what we need and need desperately. We have no iron lung in our whole section of Nigeria. Two years ago we lost a missionary who might have been saved from polio, and I don't know how many Africans have died as a result of complete paralysis of the respiratory system."

"Save us the clinical details, doctor," and Wigle put up a hand in a mock protest.

"Sorry," laughed Bill. "I'll use laymen's language from now on."

Then seriously, he said: "Polio is rare out our way, but when it hits it hits hard and is one hundred per cent fatal — at least in the cases I have known in the past five years. I think an iron lung that can also be manually operated. . . ." he stopped, then smacked his fist on the table.

The others looked at him.

"It would have to be *entirely* manual," he explained his sudden pause. "We have no electricity nor power unit on the station. I guess I've been too long away from the bush," and he was apologetic. "Perhaps we should forget about the lung for awhile."

"Power? You mean a generating plant?" queried the other man. "Look, I told you I've been in the hatchery business for a quarter of a century. Do you know that I had to rig up my own emergency plant at the hatchery? Whenever the rural power went off: I would have lost thousands of chicks if I didn't have an emergency power to switch on immediately. Would a diesel power plant do the job for you?"

"Would it!" said Bill, almost ecstatically. "It would light the hospital, help me to get some power equipment, give me light for surgery . . ." his mouth kept working but no words came out.

Jane's laughter pealed out, and soon the other three joined her.

"Oh Bill," she gasped between gusts of laughter that could not be controlled. "You looked like a little boy in a candy shop, told to take whatever he wanted," and again she went off in peals of laughter.

Bill looked sheepish, then grinned again. "I guess my imagination was running away from me," and he turned to his friend. "You shouldn't do things like that to a missionary doctor, starved for the equipment that would help to do a topnotch job. Sorry for the enthusiasm."

"Sorry nothing," and Wigle was excited. "At last I'm getting my teeth into something, and the whole thing seems to be of a pattern." He began to tick the items off on his fingers, his breakfast entirely forgotten.

"We get an iron lung. . . ." He stopped and looked at the doctor. "Isn't there a lung that a person wears when they are being moved?" When the other nodded dazedly, he went on: "Then we will get the *two* pieces, plus a power plant package." He rubbed his hands gleefully. "Let's see, I'll need a complete layout of the hospital, the houses. . . ."

"Houses!" Jane almost shrieked. "You mean we will have lights and — and — Bill, you told me I would be using lamps and wood stoves," and she turned on him in mock indignation.

"You will, you will," he replied airily. "Remember that none of this stuff is even ordered yet. It may be months before we even see it, and then it has to be set up. I only hope we can get someone who knows what to do," he said, turning to Mr. Wigle.

"As I was saying before I was interrupted," went on the man imperturbably, "the hospital, the houses, the hatchery — "

"The *hatchery?*" This time it was Bill's turn to shout.

"Yes, didn't I tell you what the second item was that came to my mind when I was praying?" he chuckled. "I've read enough about the Point Four program and the Peace Corps and every other means used to help needy people around the world. I imagine you have an educational program?" he asked Bill. When the other nodded, he went on: "Then you need a good agricultural program too. And you should start with chickens and other livestock."

"But who . . . ?" Bill interrupted.

"But *me,*" chuckled the man. "I haven't much to boast about," he went on, "but I do count my chickens before they are hatched, and I don't very often miss."

"Merle is the best hatchery man in the east." His wife was watching her spouse proudly. Then, as though it had suddenly come to her, she gasped: "You mean live on a mission station and do some work?" her eyes opened wider and wider.

"If McAdams will let us," replied her husband, and he turned to Bill.

"*Phew!*" was the reply of the doctor, "this is all too fast for me. From an iron lung to a hatchery seems to be a big step. Let's get away from the table and get up where we can breathe and talk freely."

The four of them rose, and the ladies climbed the slightly rolling gangway, the men following. Once on deck, they made their way to the deck chairs, chained securely to their guard rail, and the deck steward hurriedly came forward to attend to them. Once seated, shaded from the hot sun that even so early in the morning gave promise of a scorching day, and looking out over the gentle roll of the Atlantic, the four settled down.

Bill and Merle Wigle were soon lost in the details of what would be needed for the new venture, and gradually page after page of the businessman's pocketbook was filled with names and measurements.

Finally he stopped. "Well," and he scratched his shock of iron gray hair, "I may be new to mission work, but I know where I am in all this. Now I want you to give me the name of the firm or people that I can contact for your lung equipment, then I'm heading up to the radio room and get going on this business."

"You mean now?" Bill was incredulous.

"I mean now, and I'm going to tell the people I want them to work on it but fast, as from yesterday," and he was the keen business man, the successful worker again. "I know where to cable for my part of the business, and I'm going to have the sweetest little power plant crated and shipped before we get off this boat," and he rose to his feet, purpose in his action.

When Bill had given him the name of the hospital supply house, he wrote it down, then excused himself, walked along the deck and climbed the outside stairs to the next deck toward the radio and cable room. Bill watched him in admiration, then suddenly felt a sense of incompleteness. As the ladies continued their conversation, Bill quietly walked to the stern of the ship. He wanted to be alone, to think over this amazing thing, and to thank God Who could still work miracles, even in the unlikely place of a shipboard acquaintance. What a boon all this would be to the work that more and more weighed on his heart and mind.

And wouldn't Baru and Chuna and all his African friends

be amazed at the miracle of "lantarki," as he had heard them
name the mysterious light that came from a battery switch.
And as he thought of his friends and his work again, Bill laughed
into the breeze. First Jane, a real help meet, now the Wigles and
their good work. His hands rested on the ship's rail, and bowing
his head on them, the missionary doctor put into words the
thanksgiving that welled up within him.

That evening, when the Wigles and McAdamses were together again, they made their plans for landing and getting the
older couple introduced into Africa.

"What I would like to do," said Wigle, "is stay down here on
the coast for awhile, or until the equipment arrives. Inci-
dentally," he went on, "I cabled my manager at the hatchery
and sent him a complete list of what I wanted and when. He
must have thought I had gone completely mad, or gotten sunstroke, or something."

"*Caffard* they call it up on the desert," interjected Bill.

"Well, whatever it is, he thinks I have it. I got a reply from
him late this afternoon."

"Fast work," said Bill smiling, seeing something new in this
man.

"I learned to work fast long ago," admitted the man, and
those that work for me work fast too. Anyway, he tells me
that he has contacted the people who installed all my equipment
for me, and they are going to let us have all the equipment at
cost, since it is for — and I quote — 'a good cause.'" He chuckled.
"I also suspect that they think it will be good for their business
with me and with others, when they are generous like this."

"Even at cost, it is going to cost plenty to ship it out and
get it through customs," said Bill worriedly.

"We'll manage," replied the other. "We crate and ship
fertile eggs and chicks all over the world. I have an idea that
our crating firm will be happy to crate something more substantial
than eggs and chickens. At least I told my man to get hold of
them for the job. And I'm sure the customs duty charges for
the hospital stuff will be small. It is something I can work on
while waiting for it to arrive. Don't worry," he patted Bill's knee,
"our outfit is set up for dealings with governments and firms
all over the world, and everything will be cared for without
a hitch. And who would have thought," he said meditatively,
"when I first started a hen house, that I would be doing this
in Africa."

He slapped his own knee. "I forgot. If I'm going to set

up a hatchery for your people, I'll need some equipment for myself. I looked after everyone else, and forgot myself," he moaned plaintively. "Now back to the cable room to burn up some more ether," and he slipped out of the lounge, leaving three people gaping at him as he went.

Five

Baru, the African evangelist, was sitting in the small, windowless, round mud hut, his eyes red rimmed from smoke and lack of sleep. Sweat poured down his black skin, making it slick and shiny and reflecting the dancing light of the small fire of corn stalks that burned in the center of the room.

He stretched out one cramped leg, then withdrew it quickly as he felt his foot knock against someone else. The room was so packed with men and women that there was scarcely space to move at all. He sighed heavily.

An old woman, wrinkled and gnarled, naked except for the usual bunch of leaves tied around her middle, was leaning over the raised platform that was the typical bed of these people. On the bed, the center of all attention, was the body of a young man, lying naked, with half a dozen great gashes on his head, legs, and chest oozing blood that puddled beneath him. Baru had heard the story several times in the hour that he had been in the hut. The young man had climbed high up in a locust bean tree, gathering the provender for his goats, when suddenly, the one who was so sure footed and agile lost his grip and came crashing down on the rocks at the base of the tree. There he had been found, unconscious, and brought to this hut.

Baru was at the mission station when he heard the drums beating out their message of the accident, and immediately he had gone to the home to see if he could help. But he was too late. The witchdoctor was ahead of him, and already any hope for recovery had gone. With sickened heart, the African had seen the cupping horns on the head, chest, and abdomen of the boy. With the usual quackery, the demons that had entered the body when it was broken must be drained off, and Baru saw the calabashes of blood that sat on the floor. With every heart beat, more blood would follow, until the last flicker of life would go out and the death rites would begin.

Baru was sick at heart. How he longed for his beloved *Likita,* the missionary, Dr. McAdams, to be with him now. How he would have taken over and perhaps saved this boy's life. The African groaned aloud.

And now the old woman, crazed with grief, as though hearing the death groans of her son, threw herself over the prostrate form. With a wrinkled forefinger, she raised one eyelid and began speaking words that could not be heard and would never be answered.

"Are you too going away?" The question was a wail. "To leave me with all the work, and me an old woman? Oh son, son, don't leave me yet. My husband is blind, all my children are gone, and now you too will leave. Oh son, son," and suddenly the voice broke into a wail that came from the depths of a despairing soul, from the depths of a broken heart. It was a wail that rose and fell, quivering and keen, carrying with it anguish such as only these people could know. Then in a paroxysm of grief she threw herself on the body of her son, rolled off and on to the floor, thrashing with arms and legs until all in her vicinity had backed away, some out of the door, and finally in utter exhaustion she lay still, moaning and whimpering like a stricken puppy.

Soon only Baru was left with the bereaved and the dead. Quietly he took a blanket from the dirt floor and threw it over the lifeless corpse. Then he tenderly lifted the old woman from the floor and carried her gently outside.

There the relatives and tribespeople of the dead boy were gathered, already passing the gourd of beer from hand to hand, already swaying to the muffled rhythm of the drums, ready for the night and day of mourning that was to be debauchery and drunkenness in an attempt to blot out the reality and the uncertainty of death.

Carefully Baru carried his burden to another hut, and laid her gently on a mud platform bed. The old woman looked up at him, wonderment in her eyes.

"It's all right, mother," the African spoke her tribal language easily, "it's all right. I will see to your son's burial, then I will come back to you and we will talk about death and life." The woman, still mute and staring in her grief, continued to look as the other slipped out of the hut.

It took no little effort to induce some of the men to leave the beer pot and begin to dig the grave, but finally they set to work, Baru doing the equivalent of all the rest put together.

When the grave was ready, Baru went again into the death hut and carefully tied the corpse in the *mayafi* blanket that had been thrown over him. Then wrapping a grass mat around him too, he picked up the corpse and eased it through the low doorway.

At his appearance, the people rushed at him, pushing him back into the hut and barring the doorway with their bodies. Baru, wise in the ways of his people, waited. Then he heard the pick-pick of a native axe on the rear wall. In a moment the mud hut wall was broken through, and a hand motioned to him to slide the body through the opening. Feet first he passed it through the opening, then climbed out after it. Before nightfall, he knew, the hole would be sealed up again and the way closed. If the spirit of the dead should seek to return, it would not be able to find the way back in, and would be forced to go off and live in the bush. Thus reasoned the tribespeople.

There was no ceremony at the graveside. The body was bundled through the narrow opening of the grave mouth, then straightened out on the long base. Across the mouth were placed short bamboo rods, then the dirt was quickly pushed back in, tramped down by bare feet, and the mourners left to return to the beer pot and the night of revelry.

Baru knew how hopeless it was to try to talk to the people. Instead he slipped back to the hut where he had left the old woman, who had been forgotten by everyone else.

Baru found her sitting on the mud bed, her claw-like hands raking down her breast, leaving bloody trails as they tore at the flesh. He quickly grabbed her hands, speaking quietly to her as he did so.

"Mother," he spoke slowly, trying to get his words past the grief that was tearing at the woman, "Mother, your son is dead. He is gone now, and weeping will not bring him back again. But Mother," he had to recapture one of the hands that had torn loose, "I want to tell you something, a story of Someone who loves you and loves me and all men. He is One who wants to take away the fear and power of death, to give you life that is forever," then, simply, he told the woman the story of Jesus Christ and His love for all people. Faithfully, but almost feeling the futility of it all, he told how the Son of God had died that all who believe might not die.

The woman looked at him, unseeing eyes now burning feverishly in their sockets. The hands he held had ceased to agitate, and as he released them, the old woman fell back with a sigh, the eyes closed, and sleep claimed her.

Baru sat for a long time, his mind a tumult of thoughts. "I have failed," he almost groaned aloud. "Oh, if only the *Likita* were here. He would have saved the boy and these people would have listened to the Gospel. But now they are blind and drunk and fearful. They will not listen. I will come back again sometime, and perhaps they will listen."

The African looked down at the woman of his own people. He saw the wrinkled skin, the toil worn hands, the shaven head, the deeply cut facial marks. "Oh God," it was a prayer that burst from a full heart, "Oh God, save these my people as You have saved me. Save them, save them," and he wept softly the tears, so strange to the African, that came from the heart that God had touched. Slowly he turned and left the hut, skirted the dancing, drunken figures, and headed for his village and the mission station. The moon rode high overhead.

Six

The lorry skidded to a halt in a cloud of dust and a rattle of loose metal and wood that made the resulting silence almost deafening. From the dilapidated cab, a broad, moon-like face was followed by a short, dumpy body, then bandy legs, with feet stuffed into an ancient pair of army boots. The owner of the body stood beside his lorry for a moment, peering through the settling dust, watching the children and adults running towards him from the nearby clutter of huts. Proudly he waited, hitching up a pair of torn and patched pants as he did so. He wore no shirt.

"Garba, Garba!" the children shrieked as they caught sight of the African who was trying to act nonchalant, "*Ka zo? Ka zo?* You have come? You have come?" they chorused in Hausa.

"*Na zo,* I have come," he replied, then in the fashion of the east he greeted each one as they came up, the salutations seeming to roll on endlessly. And all the while he stood proudly at the door of the wreck he had driven, conscious of the jealous looks of the other young men who did not drive a lorry.

When the salutations were finished, the people poured in, through and under the lorry, examining the mechanical marvel that so rarely came to their part of the country. And to think that one of their own people was the driver! Pride knew no bounds.

Garba felt a whack on his shoulder and spun around. Peering over the stake body of the lorry was the wide, smiling face of his older brother.

"*Baru!*" he shouted in unmistakable glee. The other jumped over the side and soon the two men were greeting each other in their true African fashion.

"My brother comes to us riding like a chief," said Baru, grinningly gesturing to the lorry. "Should we salute you as the lion of the village, the elephant of the forest, the king of the world?" Garba responded to the mockery in the voice by giving his

35

shorts another hitch, then feeling something in his pocket he
recalled his mission. Putting his hand through one of the many
rents, he pulled out a letter, the envelope smudged and wrinkled,
and with a flourish he handed it over to Baru.

"I am no king, lion, nor elephant," and he mimicked his
brother's voice. "I am the bearer of good news for you I hope,"
and he indicated the letter.

Baru looked down at the envelope, turning the letter over
and over in his yellow-palmed hands. Never would he get
accustomed to receiving a letter, nor, from the gaze of the family
that was now on him, would his people.

"It's the paper that speaks," he heard one wisely tell another. "This is the way words are carried without the voice,"
said another. They pressed in closely, eagerly watching as he
held the letter tentatively in his hand.

He noticed the postmark on the stamp, the "kain sarki," the
monarch's head that in some mysterious way brought a letter
from afar. The country's postmark was familiar to him, and he
looked at his friends.

"*Daga Kanada,*" he said, indicating the post mark, "it is from
Canada."

Then his eagerness overcame him, and he tore at the envelope, his thick fingers producing a jagged tear as he did so. Unfolding the letter, he quickly scanned it, then slowly he began
to read it. It was written in Hausa.

"It is from *Mai Gida,* Mr. Dunning," he said, as they watched
him hopefully. He pronounced it "Meesta Dooning," then slowly
he began to read the letter aloud.

*To Baru, my faithful friend and brother in the Lord Jesus
Christ, greetings. I salute you, your wife and children, Garba*
— and he shot a grin over at his beaming brother — *and all the
believers in the church. The grace of the Lord Jesus Christ be
with you.*

*After these greetings, I have some news, some good news
that will make you very happy. The doctor is on his way to
Africa,* and as he read these words the people broke into a buzz of
comment.

"*Madalla, madalla,*" repeated Garba. "Wonderful! Thank
the Lord!" and for the first time he moved away from his cab
door and came closer to his brother. The latter went on reading.

*The doctor is on his way back to Africa, and should be ar-
riving on the great boat, the* Abosso, *about the tenth day of
May.* The reader broke off and did some quick calculating.

"It is now April the twentieth," he pronounced the name "Afril," "there remains only two weeks." He sucked in his lower lip and began chewing on it characteristically. Then he returned to the letter.

I don't know if you can make it or not, he went on, *but I think that Dr. McAdams would be very happy to see you if you can catch the road to Lagos and meet the boat. He will be driving a motor back to the mission station, and you could come back with him and his new wife.* Again the buzz of conversation stopped him. "His new wife, his new wife," and the eyes of all gleamed at the thought of their beloved physician returning to them with a wife.

If you cannot, the letter went on, *at least you will know that they will be arriving shortly. I will be following him in about a month or two, when I have finished some business here.*

My words are finished. Greet everyone for me. My eyes long to see you, and I pray for you every day. I am your friend and brother in the Lord Jesus Christ, Peter Dunning. Baru finished the letter, stood looking at it for a moment, and then folded it back into its envelope.

Quickly he spoke to his brother. "How did you get this letter, Garba? Why did it not come in the mail?"

The younger man felt important. "When I was in Jos, I got the job of bringing this *mota* to Bauchi and load it with peanuts. When I heard I was coming near my home, I visited the big mission house and asked the man there if there was anything he wanted to come out here. He gave me this letter which he said he thought might be important, since he knew that the *Likita,* the Doctor, was coming back soon. I have brought you the letter and the good news," and again his moon-like face beamed.

"When do you return?" he was asked.

"As soon as I get the bags of peanuts loaded," he replied. "I was told I must come quickly. They promised me a 'dash' to my pay if I am fast," and he swelled noticeably.

"Good," replied Baru. "And when you return, I will go to the railway with you, and go down and meet my brother at the big boat," and the loyal Baru threw his arm affectionately around Garba's shoulder.

"*To,*" replied the other. "So, I go now, and will return tomorrow or the next day. Be ready for me." Then saluting his family again, he climbed importantly into the cab, eventually got it started, and with the rattle and clang that had heralded his coming, he rolled off in a cloud of dust, a whooping group of children following as closely as they dared.

Baru watched him out of sight, then turned toward his home to make his own preparations for the long, and for him, somewhat frightening trip to the coast. It would be the farthest he had ever been away from his own home.

Seven

Packed and excited, Bill and Jane watched the boat move slowly up the great lagoon. The mangrove trees that lined the shore seemed to grow right out of the water, and whistling in and around them were birds of every size and color, singing, darting, scintillating and sparkling with myriad colors. The girl was fascinated.

Then the lagoon narrowed, the breeze of the ocean was cut off, and heat, oppressive and heavy, seemed to fall like a pall. Jane felt the sweat beginning to trickle down her face . . . and looked up at her husband. He was oblivious to everything except the scene before him, and she didn't know what to look at: his face with its reflection of emotion, or the shore where figures were beginning to come into focus as faint noises stole over the water.

The boat continued its majestic way, soon edging along the great piles of the wharf, dotted with galvanized iron sheds. People began to run back and forth, and Jane saw some of Bill's pictures coming alive before her eyes.

Dressed in tattered shorts, some with shirts, some bare chested and dark, the men waited, poised to grab the rope that would soon be sent whistling their way. Pulling it in, they dragged the heavy hawser attached to the end of it, and soon the ship was fast to the wharf, its engines stilled and the bustle of people on board filling the noise vacuum.

Jane looked up at Bill. He stood, his mouth open, and looking so ludicrous that she laughed aloud. His mouth started to work, but nothing came out. Then, almost with an effort, she heard him say:

"*Baru!* If that isn't Baru, I'll eat his fez!"

Jane followed his pointing finger, and there, head thrown back and eyes scanning the passenger lined rail, was the man of whom she had heard so much and whose picture was vivid in her memory. He was a short, bandy-legged man, dressed in long white trousers and a toga-like shirt. His head was almost completely shaven, the round, red fez perched on a kinkly poll. His round face shone with excitement as he continued to search for a familiar figure.

"Baru!" the booming voice beside her made Jane jump . . . then she was watching the African as his eyes focussed on the place where the call had come from, squinted for a moment, then suddenly his mouth split his pumpkin-like face in a great grin of recognition, and his hand came up to wave self-consciously in an unaccustomed greeting.

Bill pulled Jane toward the gang plank, almost impolite in his haste now to get ashore. It seemed hours before their passports were examined, their visas stamped, and they were free to go.

Running to keep up with him, the girl sped down the gangplank in time to see her husband take the African in a great bear-hug that fairly made his ribs creak.

Then holding him off at arm's length, he began to speak to him, and Jane felt for the first time the pangs of jealousy that she could not share in the rapid fire conversation.

As though suddenly remembering her, Bill turned back, drew her closer and introduced her to the African.

The black face was still split by the grin. As she put out a friendly hand, he took it in his and awkwardly shook it.

"Shaking hands isn't the usual method of greeting here," said Bill, "but he also says that he wants to greet you a thousand times, and to welcome you to his country." He turned back to Baru and said something to him, then back to his wife to translate the question and answer.

"I asked him how he knew when we would get here, and he said he received a letter from Peter Dunning telling him the date that the boat was due. He got out to the railroad in a lorry with his brother, then came down here by the 'fire canoe' as he called the train, the *jirgin wuta*. He arrived yesterday, and has been down on the dock here all day, just waiting for us."

He stopped to speak as Baru put his hand into a capacious pocket and pulled out a letter which he handed to McAdams.

"From Peter," he said, slitting the envelope with his finger. "Baru picked it up at the mission headquarters in Jos." He pulled out the light, airmail sheets of paper and quickly scanned them.

"Whooppee!" for a moment he looked as though he wanted to dance a jig. "Peter says that there is a nurse who has been accepted and should be flying out within a month. Now that is good news. . . ." and he turned to translate it to the African.

By this time the crowds on the wharf were thinning, and Bill remembered his goods in the customs shed. Alternating talking Hausa and English, he took the arms of his wife and his companion, and moved toward the great doors of the customs building, piled high with goods. He was back in Africa — all was right with the world!

Eight

The station wagon pulled up and billowing dust settled around it in great clouds. As the dust settled, Jane found her heart beating with strange excitement. Packed in dense rows around the vehicle were Africans of every size and shade, from coal black to light tan. They had one thing in common: an intense excitement that gave vent in such chattering that nothing and no one seemed coherent. Jane looked at her husband.

Bill was still hunched over the steering wheel, his white-knuckled hands clutching it fiercely, while down his cheeks stole tears that overflowed from brimming eyes. Then he shook his head and, slowly clambering out of the car, was immediately engulfed in a flood of humanity that swallowed him up.

"*Likita! Likita Mai Magani! Mai Magani! Sannu Bature, sannu Mai Gida!*" over and over again the names rolled out: "Doctor! Doctor! Greetings white man, greeting father," and with each salutation Bill McAdams had a reply, a pat on the head, occasionally throwing his arms around someone in an effusion of joy.

Jane was fascinated by it all, then slowly began to feel forgotten and left out. Hesitating for a moment, she opened the car door and slowly climbed out. There was an instant hush, and Bill spun around apologetically.

"I'm so sorry, darling!" His arm was through hers and he was pulling her toward the group. "Can you believe it, but I almost forgot you. What a reception for the doctor's bride. Do forgive me."

"Don't be foolish," she looked up at him with pride. "I'm just so glad that I can share all this with you, and share you with them," and she sent a beaming smile over the group. Immediately the salutations poured over her, Bill vainly striving to interpret them all, first into English and then back into Hausa. It was bedlam.

42

At last order was restored and Baru took charge of unloading the station wagon, while willing hands carried boxes and bags over to the mission house. And for the first time Jane had a good look at the place that was to be her home for the next four years.

She saw the whitewashed walls and pan roof, and the great shutters raised over the windows to keep out the hot glare of the tropical sun. Then with Bill eagerly pulling her along, she went through the doorway and entered what was evidently the living room. The plainness of it surprised her, then she remembered the four years of bachelorhood, and suddenly she laughed and flung herself into the arms of her husband, who was standing back and watching her with his heart in his eyes and a question forming on his lips.

"Oh Bill," she hugged him, "I think it's wonderful. Wait until I get some of our things unpacked and it will be a real home — *our* home," she added with emphasis.

He breathed a great sigh. "Thank the Lord!" He looked around. "I was afraid that you would be disappointed. Guess I didn't spend too much time fixing it up, then I left in such a hurry when the leopard clawed my arm, and I guess it just isn't a place to bring a bride to." The words kept tumbling out of his mouth as though he was trying to get everything off his mind at once.

Just then the men came in with bags and boxes, and the two began to find places for them until they could be unpacked.

In a few minutes she missed Bill, and looking out the door saw him walking with Baru up the short hill to where another large whitewashed building stood.

The hospital, and he can't wait to get into it, she said to herself, and smiled at her man. Then the smile froze on her face. Racing down the hill came a flying wedge of men, feathered headdresses flying in the breeze, spears waving over their heads, and shrieks and shouts coming in such unison that her blood seemed to freeze in her veins.

Helplessly she watched as they reached the doctor, surrounded him with the same wild shouting and waving of spears, until he was lost in the midst of the flying legs and waving plumes. Suddenly she wanted to be beside him, and she flung out of the doorway and raced up the short hill. Then she saw Bill, grinning and shouting in the middle of the wild melee, pointing first to this one then that one among the dancers.

Jane felt a hand on her arm, and standing beside her was a little girl, looking shyly up at her.

"Hello." The oddly phrased word came out as a short "haylow" from the African girl's lips. Again, as though trying to communicate, she added: "Okay," then shyly dropped her eyes. In a warmth of friendliness, Jane impulsively put her arm around the girl and hugged her tightly. Just then Baru moved over toward her, his eyes twinkling. Saying something she could not understand, he swung his arm toward the dancers, and she saw that they were moving in perfect rhythm and pattern round and round her husband. Then the movement slowed, and finally stopped, and she heard Bill talking to them, gesticulating in the way that she knew so well. Finally he broke through the circle and came to her.

"This is my day to apologize," he said on reaching her side. "But I know you will understand. Baru here, the rascal, told me I was needed right away at the hospital. I thought it was an emergency, the way they all are when I am here, so I came right up. He knew that these men were coming down from the town, and he wanted me to get the full benefit of it. I'm afraid we haven't grown used to having a woman on the place" — here he grinned his infectious smile — "but we will eventually. Hey, I see you have a friend already," and he knelt down in front of the little girl. "This is Baru's daughter. He dug her name out of the New Testament and calls her Biriskilla. It's Hausa for Priscilla. We call her Biscuits around here," and he chucked the girl under the chin.

"Hello," she said, looking up at him impishly, "Okay."

Bill howled, and standing up swung the little girl to his shoulder. "Who has been teaching you English?" he asked with mock severity in that tongue. "And you have forgotten how to speak Hausa?"

The girl squealed with fear, both at the position high up on his shoulder and at his tone. He swung her down again. Then speaking to her in her own tongue he said: "Biriskilla, how would you like to help *Uwar gida* here?" and he motioned to his wife. "She doesn't know your language yet, and there are so many things for her to learn about your country. I will be busy at the hospital" — he called it "asibiti" — "and she will need someone. Will you be her 'teacher'?"

Biriskilla looked up at the tall man who spoke to her so seriously. "*Likita*," she said in like manner to his, "I am only a little girl. But if Mother here would like me to be her *kawata*, her close friend, I will be happy."

Bill turned to tell his wife about the conversation. She responded in kind, "Tell her that she will be the daughter of the house," she said, "and if her father agrees, she can help me as I learn to live here."

The conversation finished, the three of them turned back to the group of men who were again chanting and beginning a shuffling dance.

"The chief is coming," whispered Bill hurriedly to Jane, then moved forward to join the people who were now all looking up the hill beyond the hospital.

Jane first saw the massive red umbrella, then as the crowd parted, she saw the man under it, his high turban almost brushed by the fringe of the shade held by one of his men. As he came through the double line of singing, shuffling dancers, he caught sight of the young doctor and his wife, the latter still holding Biriskilla's hand.

With an imperious gesture he waved the escort back and then, alone, approached the missionaries.

"My brother," and he stretched out a long, trim hand to the doctor, "my brother, I welcome you back to your home. We have long waited for you to return, and now our stomachs are white because you are here.

"And you," he turned to Jane, "you too we welcome as the mother of the house of the mission. I see you already have taken the hand of one of my people," and he looked down smilingly at the little girl. "This is the way your husband has always been with us." He paused while Bill interpreted his words. Then he continued: "There was a day long ago when we did not want your husband or your God. Today I welcome you both in the name of your God and mine. We are brothers, and I too would hold your hand." Then in almost childish simplicity he took Jane's free hand and one of Bill's and held them for a moment. "Let me know your needs. But for now I have a few gifts." Dropping their hands, he clapped his own, and there pushed forward a group of men and women, each one bearing a load on his head.

There were great clusters of bananas, some ripe, some green. There were baskets of yams, the large tubulars piled like cordwood and threatening to topple at any moment.

Some of the women brought chickens, their feet tied with grass rope, and others came forward with eggs and pineapples.

One man led a fat, bleating goat, and stood by the pile of gifts to indicate that this too belonged to the new arrivals.

Jane's head whirled as she saw the pile grow higher and higher, while for each one she heard her husband's: *"Mun gode, ai mun gode dayawa. . . .* Thank you, thank you a thousand times."

Finally the gifts came to an end, and once more Bill spoke his thanks to the chief. Then it was over, and Bill and Jane were left with Baru and Biriskilla looking down at the food and the fowl and the still bleating goat.

Bill chuckled, then suddenly laughed. Jane looked at him for a moment, then she too began to laugh, joined by the deep chuckle of Baru and the childish treble of Biriskilla.

"I — I — I — " Bill was trying to speak between gusts of laughter, "I — I didn't know whether to laugh or to cry, so I decided it was better to laugh. Will you stuff the goat for dinner tonight?" he looked at Jane and then went off into another fit of laughter.

When he had control of himself, he took the goat's tether, and with a word to Baru to ask some of the men to help bring the gifts into the kitchen, he headed back for the house. Jane and Biriskilla followed.

Nine

"Hi, Prof!" the voice rang down the corridor of the school. A tall, dark man, his thinning hair showing just a touch of gray at the temples, spun around at the all too familiar greeting. His eyes were glinting behind his heavy, rimmed glasses. At the sight of his visitor, the sharp look was replaced with one of intense delight.

"Peter!" he exclaimed, his pleasure showing in voice and face as he strode down the hall to meet the other, "where did you come from?"

"Oh, wandering up and down and to and fro on the earth," he quoted with a grin, "although I assure you I have an entirely different purpose than the one who used the words originally. I just called in at the school here hoping that I would find you before you left for home."

"I live here — practically," the teacher said with a grimace. "Home is where my hat is, and it hangs here most of the time," and he banged that unoffending article with his fist. "But tell me," and he grabbed the arm of the tall, fair young man whose eyes, set in a tanned, pleasant face, crinkled with sheer delight at seeing his friend again, "you've been away for months, and I haven't seen or heard from you since Bill and Jane McAdams were married. How about dinner with me? That is, if you can stand a bachelor dinner — which means a frozen one. Heated for you of course," he added playfully.

"Good idea," replied Peter Dunning. "Just let me phone Ruth first and I'm with you. Besides," and he gave his friend a queer look, "there are some things I would like to talk over with you."

They walked down the school corridor together, stopping at the office where Peter made the call to his wife. Then the two left the school and stepped out into the chill of the early evening.

On the street Dunning stopped. He looked back at the gray-stone building they had just left.

"Good old Melbourne College," he spoke affectionately. "It scarcely seems ten years since I graduated. And you, Prof," and he put his arm affectionately around the shoulder of his friend, "you don't look a day older than when Bill and I used to spend the evening in your apartment and plan our futures," and he laughed boyishly, the crinkles around his eyes coming out in sharp relief.

The two stood in silence for a few minutes, then turned and started down to the parking lot. Still silent they climbed into the teacher's car and headed for his apartment.

He parked his car in the allotted slot, then the two took the small elevator to the fourth floor and walked the long, carpeted hall to the apartment. While they stood in front of the door and his friend sought the proper key on his ring, Peter looked around idly. The air of quiet well-being was apparent in the wall-to-wall broadloom, in the quiet tones of wall and ceiling, the hidden lighting. Then his eyes returned to his friend who was inserting the key in the door, just below the illuminated name plate: Michael Woods, M.Sc., B.Paed. Then the door was open, a light flashed on, and the two men entered the room.

Peter looked around quickly. The place was the same he had known for years, the quiet home of the dedicated teacher, the place where he and countless others had been privileged to come and talk to a man who would listen to boyish hopes and dreams, and one who was wise enough to counsel them well.

"Remember our first visit here?" asked Peter.

"I surely do," replied the other, "you and Bill McAdams, and never will I forget how you two introduced me to life with a purpose," and he smiled at the memory. "And when I saw what Christ meant to you two as young students, I can still remember the hunger I had to know Him too. And speaking of hunger," and he chuckled, "I'd better start de-freezing our dinner. Make yourself comfortable," and he disappeared into his small kitchen.

He was back almost immediately. "This is real, rugged pioneer life," and he mopped his forehead in mock fatigue, "we have to put the dinners in the oven so they can defrost and get warm," and he threw himself into an easy chair with a chuckle.

He looked around his well-appointed apartment. "This is a little different from the mission house that Bill and I found raided by the leopard men when we visited you five years ago," he remarked casually. But as he did so there flashed into his memory, as so often happened to him now, the scenes of the visit that he and young Dr. McAdams had paid to Dunning and the hidden valley, and the rescue of the missionary from the ancients among the leopard men.° The two men were silent as though the same picture had flashed into their minds simultaneously.

They remained silent for so long that finally Peter looked up with a grin.

"Prof," the other drew his eyes away from the fireplace and looked across at his friend, "why have you never married?"

"Never saw the girl I would want to share my life with," he spoke offhandedly, but Peter heard the undercurrent of regret in his voice. "If I ever saw that someone, it wouldn't take me long. In the meantime, I'm married to my art," and he struck a simpering pose that brought mocking laughter from his friend.

Again there was silence. Both knew that there was something under the surface that had not been mentioned.

"Look, Mike," and for one of the few times in their long friendship, Peter dropped the old and familiar schoolboy nickname, "I want to have a talk with you, and I'll eat much better after I'm finished. Do you mind?"

"Not at all," replied Woods. "I can see you've got something bottled up inside of you, so get it out and make room for my own brand of home cooked dinner," and he settled back in his leather-covered chair and waited.

Instead of settling back, Dunning got to his feet and began to pace up and down in front of his friend, his chin tucked low, as though seeking some way to begin. There was no easy way, so almost blurting it out, he said: "Mike, are you tied to Melbourne College? Would you consider leaving it?" and he waited almost breathlessly, as though the whole future hinged on the answer.

Woods looked up at the slim young man towering over him, and saw the intensity of the look on his face. "Well," he almost drawled the answer, "I'm really not married to this place," and he swept his arm around what was definitely a man's room. He chuckled, "I'm not married to the school nor to this apartment. But having taught there for fifteen years, I wouldn't just drop out without some good and valid reasons. So start naming them."

Again the other man was silent for a moment. He seemed

° As told in *Hidden Valley* by the same author.

to be praying and groping for the right words. Then finally it all came out in a rush.

"You have been to Africa," and the teacher nodded, "and know something of our work. Since your visit there you have supported it with money, prayer, and interest, so that in a very real sense you are a partner with Bill and me in what is being done." Again the other nodded. This was exactly his feeling.

"Well," continued Dunning, "since you were there we have opened a hospital, and in about a month Bill and Jane will be back there and it will be in full swing again. In another six months I will also be back there and will be trying to get around to some of the villages where we were never able to go before." His brow was knitted as though he felt his thoughts and words were getting mixed up. "You also know something of the recent problems in Africa, with the increasing demand for independence and a voice and a place among the nations of the world. I'm all for it," he went on almost fiercely, "and I'm hoping to have a share in helping the people realize their goal. But so many of them are not ready for the cataclysmic upheaval that follows the removing of all outside help, and I personally feel that the only surety for a stable future for Africa is to see that its people get independence in the context of Christianity. If this is not so, I don't know what is going to happen. Africa will lie open, and could be the richest prize on earth for anyone who can conquer her." The man paused for breath.

"Oh, it's too long and complicated," he went on, finally, "but I do feel that what we do as missionaries in the next few years is going to be vitally important to Africa and to the world. And I think that most of all it is going to be vitally important to the future of the Church of Christ in Africa, and perhaps the whole of the eastern world.

"Anyway," he went on, "I am laying some plans that I feel will help Africans and will help our work to this end. And one of the big aids to help will be education. They have a church; they have a hospital; now we feel that we must also give them a school — in a real sense, Christian education. And since English will be the language of freedom for the people, as one African told me, we are going to need someone to teach, and to teach in English.

"Mike," and he strode over and stood above his friend, then dropped his hand to his shoulder with a strong clutch and said slowly: "I have been praying constantly about this, and each time your face and name come to mind. I may be wrong, but I feel I must ask you: Mike, will you join Bill and Jane and Ruth and me on our mission station and open and teach a school for African young people? You've visited us. You know what to expect." His eyes went around the room significantly, then came back to Michael Woods, and there was almost a feverish look in them as he waited.

Michael felt the grip on his shoulder, but more he felt a burning sensation in his own throat. There flashed through his mind all that he had, then superimposed over the picture was a vision of the stark mission station, the heat he had known, the people, so backward, sometimes so fierce and cruel. Back and forth, back and forth, his mind raced, seeking to take in every facet of both situations.

Finally, swallowing to lubricate his throat, he said slowly: "Peter, you and I both know that something like this cannot be decided by either you or me. Perhaps you have prayed about it, and spoken out of a full heart. You must know what it means to me to even consider it. Give me some time, and I'll let you know when I feel a decision has been made."

The other smiled. "That's all I want," and he slapped Mike on the shoulder he had been gripping. "Just give God a chance to speak to you, and I'll be satisfied with His decision. Now let's eat," and he headed for the kitchen, followed, more slowly, by the teacher.

It was while they were eating that Peter spoke of another reason for his visit to the school. "Tomorrow night I have to speak to a group of students, and I was wondering if you would like to come along. Another dose of missions won't hurt you," he said slyly, "and these are special students. There is a missionary conference, and this is a special student night, and I understand that there will be a large group from the Bible college there — my old alma mater," and he kissed his fingers in a mock salute. "Come along and keep me company."

"Young people," said the other in dismay, his fingers tracing the line of graying hair at his temple. "Young people — me?"

"Young as you feel," replied Dunning, "and besides I need someone to support me," and he reflectively stroked the blond hair that would never gray.

"If it's support you need, of course I'll come along," replied Woods, and he turned his attention to his dessert.

Ten

The man watched the shadows dancing on the wall as the flame of the fireplace rose and fell, set in motion by its own heat. And as he watched, he felt the same sense of burning within himself. For he knew what his answer to Peter Dunning must be. Not for a single day, since his visit to Africa with Bill McAdams to see their old friend Peter Dunning, had he known the sense of quiet and accomplishment with which he had spent his first few years in teaching.

He hadn't told Dunning of the constant unrest that he had felt. Nor did he mention that at the first suggestion of what was in his visitor's mind, he had known what his own answer must be. But he also knew that no impetuous answer would do for the rugged new life and uncertain years that would lie ahead should he go to Africa.

"To go or not to go? Is this the way for me?" over and over again the questions rang, and each time he felt that he must shout a "yes, yes," although no one would hear but himself.

Suddenly he spun around from his chair and dropped to his knees. Then humbly and simply he prayed: "Oh God, I thank You for ever sending Peter Dunning my way, and for his leading me to find in Your Son, my Saviour. I do thank You for what I have known of Your love and care, and for what I have seen of Your work in Africa. And now, if Peter has spoken tonight as Your voice to me, help me to know it. Don't let me make a mistake in doing Your will and working out Your purpose for my life. Make me sure, and then help me to do what must be done." Then with a sigh he rose to his feet. *What next?* he wondered.

The next morning he awoke, tired and restless. Sleep had been fleeting, and he showered and shaved with a feeling of great depression. Somehow, he had to get an answer, and he didn't know where to turn next.

The school day went by on leaden feet, and his beloved science classes seemed a bore, the students a group of clods, and it was with relief that he found himself shutting the door of the laboratory at the end of the day.

He was walking down the main corridor when the principal's voice stopped him.

"Oh Mike, do you have a minute?" and he saw the portly principal standing at the door of his office, beckoning him in. The teacher went over, dreading the thought of trying to talk to the "Head" in his present mood. As he neared, he saw he had a sheaf of papers in his hand.

"Mike," the principal fanned out the papers he had in his hand, "I wonder if you will look these over for me and tell me what you think of them? They came in the mail today, and I would like to have your opinion," and he pressed the papers into Mike's unresisting hands. Then with a wave, he turned back into the office, evidently not noticing the attitude of the taciturn teacher.

Mike looked at the papers with unseeing eyes, then stuffing them into his pocket, he left the building, headed for the parking lot and his car. He wanted to get home and think.

On reaching his apartment, he took off his jacket, and as he did he felt the thick packet of papers in the pocket. Idly he took them out and laid them on the small table by the door, went over to the cupboard and hung up his coat.

Still idly moving, he walked back to the door, picked up the papers and moved over to his easy chair. He felt he could think better there than anywhere.

He sat down and began turning the papers over in his hand. Then words and sentences caught his eye:

"EXCHANGE TEACHERS WANTED! We no longer live in an isolated world. Let us share the good things of our life with those who have little. Teachers are being sought who will give two years to teach in other countries. Share your knowledge, your life with others. Teacher exchange can be arranged for Europe, India, Africa. . . . Africa. . . . Africa. . . . Africa. . . ." the word seemed to be written out over and over again before the fascinated gaze of the teacher. "Africa. . . . Africa. . . . will you go to Africa, Mike?" It was the voice of Peter. And suddenly he knew.

With an exclamation, he dropped the papers and went to the telephone. He was calling Peter.

Eleven

The hall was crowded with young people, and some not so young, Woods saw with a sense of satisfaction as he and Peter entered the door. On seeing Dunning, a young man came up and introduced himself as the president of the group. Peter in turn introduced him to Michael Woods. Then, excusing themselves, the two went to the platform, while the teacher found a seat near the back of the room.

The program was similar to many that he had attended since becoming a Christian: song service, prayer, special music, and the inevitable announcements. All very prosaic and orderly, and the teacher settled himself down into his seat to wait for his friend to be through so that they could go off and talk.

He glanced up when Peter Dunning was being introduced. It was a little flowery, and he smiled to himself as he realized the impatience that his friend always showed at such times. He saw Peter, his legs crossed, hand covering his mouth, waiting out the ordeal, the only sign of perturbation being the almost ceaseless pumping of his left foot as it hung over his right knee. When the introductions were finished, he rose slowly to his feet and, flipping his Bible open on the stand, he waited quietly for a moment. Then, "Let us all pray," and with a rustle heads were bowed, movement ceased, and Peter began to pray.

"Dear Heavenly Father, we come into Thy presence in the Name and through the work of the Lord Jesus Christ. We thank Thee for Him and all that He means to us, saving us and making us Thy children through faith in Him. We pray that tonight it will be the Lord Jesus Christ who is honored here; that it will be the Lord Jesus Christ whose voice is heard; that it will be the claims of the Lord Jesus Christ that we will consider. May He in all things have the preeminence. And now Heavenly Father," the voice paused for an instant, "Thy Word lies open before us. May our hearts lie open to Thy Word. Do Thou speak to us from these pages. Take this Word, this holy seed that Thou hast given to us, and plant it in our hearts.

54

Then water it by the working of Thy Holy Spirit, and cause Thy Word to be fruitful in us. We pray for Jesus' sake, Amen."

Another rustle and the audience straightened, looking up intently at this bronzed, blonde man who stood so tall and straight before them. Then, his eyes twinkling, he began to speak to them, easily, fluently, but with an underlying seriousness that seemed to settle on all.

"I was glad to receive the invitation to speak to your group on this last meeting of the conference," he began. "When the president phoned me," and he turned to acknowledge him still sitting on the platform a little to one side, "he said he wanted me to be the last speaker. It sounded like the last straw," and the young people gave an appreciative chuckle. "It reminded me of the day before I was to be married in Africa, when, like most prospective bridegrooms, I was fidgety and nervous, wishing there was some painless (and inexpensive) way of getting married. Mr. Woods of Melbourne College, who came here with me tonight, will vouch for all this, since he was with me, and in fact gave my wife away in the absence of her father." Several pair of eyes glanced searchingly around the audience, then returned to the speaker.

"The morning before I was to be married, I was having my devotions as usual — a practice that I recommend to all of you, whether you plan or hope to get married or not." Another chuckle went around the room.

"That morning I was reading in the New Testament in the first epistle of Peter, chapter four, and as usual I also read one of the modern translations. At that time I was using Moffatt's translation of the New Testament. When I turned to see how he would say it, I found in verse four these words: *Now the end of all things is at hand.*" The young people laughed, and he waited until they subsided. Then he went on: *"The end of all things is at hand. Steady then, keep cool, and pray."* The young people howled, and the teacher chuckled as he heard again Peter's account of the event.

When the laughter had died down, Peter looked down at the young people, then very simply he said: "Young people, in life you need to keep cool, real cool, and pray. Unless you do, and unless it is real with you, life can be an awful mess. But what is prayer unless you have Someone to pray to? And very simply tonight, I want to talk to you about how you can have Someone by your side all the time, in any circumstance, anywhere. And that One is the Lord Jesus Christ. If you have your

Bible, and you will need the Old Testament for this, turn with me to the first book of Samuel, chapter fourteen. There is a story here that tells how you can have Someone with you, and what it means to have Him as your Companion, your Guide, your Friend." Then with beautifully clear diction and enunciation, Peter read the story of Jonathan and his armor bearer and their exploits against the whole Philistine army. He finished the story and laid the Bible down on the stand again.

"There are two people involved in this story, Jonathan and his armor bearer," he began. "Tonight we will think of Jonathan as an illustration of the Christian. The armor bearer is the Companion and Guide to whom I would introduce each one of you tonight, the Lord Jesus Christ.

"There are several highlights to this story, and these will be my message to you.

"Notice in the first verse that Jonathan 'told not his father.' I suppose that some critics would say that this is a denial of a basic Bible commandment. For we are told to 'honor thy father and thy mother.' And I say it is true. The young person who deliberately and wilfully dishonors his parents, who has no respect for them and their authority in the home, will know something of the punishment that comes from God who has established this moral law.

"But in our story tonight, we find that the father, King Saul, is out of fellowship with God and has himself wilfully disobeyed God. Paul told Timothy that young people should 'honor their parents in the Lord' and there comes a time when the young person, honestly and before God, must make a decision for himself or herself, and do it alone, privately, quietly.

"You are responsible to God for yourself and your decisions. You are responsible to God for what you do with your life and your talents. And you must make two decisions that no one else can make for you, nor can anyone stop you from making them.

"The first decision must be made because Jesus Christ died for you, putting away your sin forever by the sacrifice of Himself. He died to save you, to be your Saviour. You must decide: Will you put your trust in the Lord Jesus Christ and be saved?

"And the second decision is: Will you obey Romans 12:1, 2: *I beseech you therefore, brethren, by the mercies of God, that ye present your bodies a living sacrifice, holy, acceptable unto God, which is your reasonable service. And be not conformed to this world, but be ye transformed by the renewing of your mind, that you may prove what is that good, and acceptable, and perfect, will of God.*

"Your bodies . . . a living sacrifice. This thing," and Peter held up his hands, waggling his fingers, touching his head, his chest and gesturing to the rest of his body. "Will I give my body, and my talents, the training this body has received, the strength of my mind, all I am and have — will I give these to Jesus Christ too? This is a decision we all must make, and we must make it alone. No one can enter into the experience of the individual with God. It is between Him and you." And the voice, which had not been raised, seemed to thunder out.

He paused for a moment. "Every example of a man meeting God, whether in the Bible or in our own day, is one of a solitary meeting. Sometimes it is in church or in a meeting like this. Sometimes it is in the quietness of our own room or in the dead of night. Somewhere, alone, we have dealings with God. And it was this experience that Jonathan could not tell his father. He had to obey God rather than man. The Philistines were boasting that they had defeated God because the people of God, under King Saul, were afraid and hiding and refusing to obey God.

"Notice that when Jonathan goes out on his journey — or his 'adventure with God' if you will — that he did not go alone. He had his armor bearer with him.

"When Jonathan asked the armor bearer to go with him, did you notice how he said: *Do all that is in thine heart. Behold, I am with thee, according to all that is in thine heart.* It wasn't just a head knowledge, or a mental impulse that was sending Jonathan out on his mission. It was heart experience, the heart where God meets men and women, instilling His own impulses, His own love, His own motives, and then making a man to do them."

He was still standing quietly behind the stand. Silently he moved to one side, his hand free and gesticulating easily. "And God is speaking to each one of you tonight. Not to your head, but to your heart, where He wants to reign and be King," and the long fingers embraced the whole room. He stepped back to the stand.

"Let us see what was involved in this adventure of a young man with his God, his Lord. And perhaps we will see some illustrations to tie to our own lives. Did you notice as I was reading that the way was not easy? It was hard, but there was a way through. The Bible tells us that they came to a great high and rocky place where there were two rocks. The name of one, in the Hebrew tongue, was Bozez, the other was Seneh. On these high and rocky slopes there were other hazards. Bozez means high. Seneh is a thorn bush. Both were designed to keep people away, to form an almost impassable barrier.

"Just south of where I live in Africa," Peter noticed how they sat up with fresh interest as he began speaking of his adopted home, "there is a great valley where we have had some amazing and wonderful experiences with a tribe of people called Kitta. Beyond their valley at its southern end, they are closed in by a great range of hills. This range is called Bima by some people, meaning 'judgment.' Others call it a name that roughly translated means 'The Tangled Mountain.' And it is tangled. Great rocks and a peculiar thorn bush make it almost impossible to cross.

"Then one day just before coming home on furlough with an arm that had been torn by a leopard, my colleague Dr. Bill McAdams heard of a narrow pass that the Africans insisted is the only way across the tangled mountain. Beyond are tribes of people who have never heard the Gospel. Dr. McAdams and I plan to go there as soon as possible. We must go and help these people. That which was impassable became passable as soon as we sought a way over, when we knew that God was leading us that way.

"Jonathan and his armor bearer were in a like situation. They could have seen the high and thorny, rocky heights and turned back in discouragement. Instead they went over their tangled mountain and had victory, because God was in it.

"Young people, I don't know what missionary service means to you. To me it means high and rocky places, difficult and hard work. There is no glamor, no ecstatic thrill just in going to another country. It is hard, difficult, and often dangerous work as we so well know." He paused. And in that pause, Michael Woods saw again that hidden valley where he and McAdams had rescued Peter Dunning from the crazed leopard men.* *Dangerous indeed*, ran through his mind. Then Peter was speaking again.

"But with our Armor Bearer, there is no place too hard, too difficult, or too dangerous. That we know too. The secret is, how does one get over the tangled mountain? Jonathan gives us a clue.

* As told in *Hidden Valley* by the same author.

"Notice near the end of the story how he and the armor bearer 'climbed up upon their hands and upon their feet.' This means two things to us:

"First it is the attitude of prayer, or worship and submission. It is not the attitude of fighting, of belligerence, of pride, of self-confidence. If he were confident he would have tried to go up in a standing position, spear in one hand and sword in the other. There was fighting to do. But he had early learned the secret of strength and power: in dependence upon God and in surrender to Him. It is His work, and His will be the victory.

"Remember the story of five young men who were martyred in South America a few years ago? And how, before going out into their dangerous work, they gathered around a small portable organ and sang:

"We rest on Thee" — our Shield and our Defender,
We go not forth alone against the foe;
Strong in Thy strength, safe in Thy keeping tender,
"We rest on Thee and in Thy Name we go."

"We rest on Thee" — our Shield and our Defender,
Thine is the battle, Thine shall be the praise;
When passing through the gates of pearly splendour,
Victors — we rest with Thee through endless days.*

"Learn that secret, and you will know something of victory that is real victory.

"But there is another lesson here. Hands are to work with, feet are to walk with. God has things for you to do, places for you to walk. It may be the sandy desert of Africa, the villages of India, or the jungle of South America. It may be the teeming cities of Europe, or the streets of your own city here. But those hands and feet, that body of yours must be surrendered as a "living sacrifice" so that He shall have it walk in His way and work at His work.

"This is the decision that you must make tonight: Will I make this surrender to Jesus Christ, or will I just live my life my own way? One way or the other, you will decide — tonight."

Dunning paused, then put his hand into his jacket pocket and drew out a light blue card. "I have here a card. On it are these words: *My Consecration: I believe that Jesus Christ died for me and that He rose again from the dead. I have trusted in Jesus Christ as my Saviour, and now I make this commitment of myself:*

* By Edith G. Cherry. By permission of Marshall, Morgan and Scott, Ltd.

Lord Jesus Christ: All I am, all I have, all I ever will be and all I ever will have, I give to Thee, absolutely, unconditionally, now and forever.

"Tonight, this card and its decision are presented to you. As we sing that beautiful hymn of consecration: 'Take my life and let it be consecrated, Lord, to Thee,' I would say: If tonight you will make this surrender to Jesus Christ, yield Him your body, mind, talents, time — your whole life, come from your seat, and in front of this group of young people take this card, sign it, and go out, knowing that you belong to Him for His service, His purpose for your life."

Dunning signalled the pianist, and slowly the strains of the hymn filled the room. Still sitting quietly, the young people followed his lead and softly began to sing. The air was tense, many eyes were on the floor, others staring straight ahead, as the verse ended. There was no movement. Peter started the next verse: *Take my will and make it Thine, it shall be no longer mine,* and just as the first line finished, there was a muffled sob, and from one side of the room there stepped a girl, her back to Mike, and she walked slowly to the front. Dunning met her, laid a card in her hand, then stood quietly singing, looking out over the group. Slowly another followed, then two young men, then a couple came, almost hesitating at each step, but finally reaching the speaker. Into each hand went a card, and the hymn continued.

Mike watched, his own heart strangely stirred. This was his memory of Peter's own response to the appeal some half dozen years before, and the memory flooded him with a soft glow. He felt as though he would have given anything to be able to join the young people at the front. Then suddenly he was out of his seat and moving slowly to the front. With tear filled eyes, Peter Dunning watched his friend walk what must have seemed an endless aisle, then very gently he was placing a card in the teacher's hand. The other young people moved slightly to make room for him in their unbroken line.

The hymn was finished. Then Peter, his hands raised in benediction, prayed. He prayed for the ones who were standing immediately in front of him, as he committed them and their dedication to God. He prayed for the rest of the audience. Then he closed: "Oh God, tonight each one of us is faced with a tangled mountain. Show us the way up and over — Thy way . . . and give us all the courage to take it. We ask it for Jesus' sake. Amen."

Twelve

Michael Woods and Peter Dunning were huddled before the fireplace in the former's apartment. Both seemed excited, and Dunning could scarcely keep his seat.

He turned to his companion: "Prof, this is the best news ever. I have never asked anyone to go to the mission field before. But somehow I felt compelled to ask you the other day. And I'm glad I did. But I'm gladder still that you didn't answer me then. What made you really decide?"

"Two things," he said. "Tonight, the tangled mountain. And something else. After you left last night," he went on, "I tried to think it all through, and got nowhere. So then I prayed and asked the Lord to do something to make me know that this was the thing that I should do. Don't mistake me," he said. "If I had the choosing, I think I would have just gone ahead. But I know that this would not be good for the work or for me. I knew the Lord had to somehow break through and show me.

"Well, yesterday, after a most miserable teaching day, I was heading home when the 'Head' called me into his office and asked me to go over some papers he had. I just took them and stuffed them into my pocket. Then when I got home, I began to read them, and found that they were a strong appeal for teachers to go to other parts of the world on an exchange basis and to help backward people. What got me was the appeal on the basis that we had something here that they needed. To me it was a sermon, although I guess the author or authors of the pamphlets might not appreciate their being called that," and he laughed. "I suddenly remembered all that I had because of the Lord Jesus Christ, then remembered all that your people in Africa did not have. Then when I saw that teachers were needed in Africa, I just felt as though a dike had burst and that this was the answer. Last night was the final lead for me.

"I spoke to the principal today, and while he didn't quite

give me his blessing, he seemed to understand what had happened to me. He was a mite sorry that I wasn't going as one of his shining lights on an exchange basis, but I guess he figured that there would be reflected glory somehow," and again he chuckled.

Dunning looked over at his friend. The tall, slim length of him was completely relaxed in his easy chair. His sparse hair was ruffled where he had run his fingers through it, and Peter saw the touch of gray at the temples. Then he saw the man watching him, a secret grin on his face.

"Do I pass inspection, O Honored Leader?" he asked mockingly.

"Sorry, Mike," replied the other, "I didn't mean to be rude. But I was just noting the prize catch, and am so grateful to God and to you that I scarcely know what to say."

"Well, I know a couple of things you can say right off," he replied. "I know my way around at the school, but I haven't a clue about this new step. So out with hints and helps to future missionaries," and he put out his hands in mock appeal.

"I've got something better than that," replied Dunning. "Tonight Ruth and I are having that group of students who came forward, in for coffee and cake and a chin wag about the future. She was especially keen that I get you to come along. After I told her about the meeting last night, she was emphatic. 'I want all the students who came forward,' she said, so consider yourself demoted," and he chuckled at the memory of his wife's comment.

"*Pro*moted you mean," replied the other. "I honestly think it would be a demotion not to be a missionary!" and he looked his new-found joy. "So take me along and introduce me as the newest and rawest of student recruits, but also as the most happy and satisfied one."

"Okay. Get dressed then and let's go." Woods went into his bedroom to dress.

The drive to Dunning's small apartment was short, and soon they were being welcomed by a radiant Ruth.

"Prof," the greeting rang with pure delight, and suddenly he felt her arms around his neck and she had kissed him. "You are more than ever a part of the family now. But surely I can kiss the man who gave me away in marriage too," and she looked lovingly at Peter who grinned down at her.

She spoke again, her voice high and gay: "Peter was so thrilled last night that he could hardly sleep. Oh this is wonderful, wonderful!" and she spun away, dragging him by the hand over to the group at the far side of the room. These were the people who, twenty-four hours before, he had not known even existed. Then last night they had stood shoulder-to-shoulder in that greatest of all acts: dedication of life to the Lord Jesus Christ. He felt a strange warmth and kinship as he moved toward them.

"Look everyone, I want you to meet Michael Woods, better known to us all as 'Prof,'" and then one by one she introduced them to her guest.

"And this is Pat Donnell," she was saying, when Michael's eyes swung from a strapping six-foot-two giant to whom he had just been introduced. Next to him and almost dwarfed as she stood back slightly, was the girl to whom he was being introduced by Ruth. For once the teacher's poise was gone. Nearly his own height, the girl was looking at him with wide, hazel eyes, frankly interested in the introduction. Mike muttered something innocuous, then found his eyes drawn again to her. *Hazel*, he said to himself, *with that little gold fleck in them*, and it was almost a physical wrench for him to take his eyes away lest he be staring too boldly.

"And it looks as though Pat feels called to our field," went on Ruth, oblivious to what was going on at her side. His heart stirred, and then feeling that his own small talk would appear foolish, he began to turn away. As he did so his heart sank, for the young giant had turned possessively to Pat and begun speaking to her in a low voice.

But as he turned, he felt a hand on his arm. "They tell me, Mr. Woods, that you are going to Africa too?" It was a question she asked. Michael tried to register the quality of her voice but it slipped away from him. It was a tone that seemed to breathe its words, rather than speak them, and he almost missed what she said.

"It rather looks that way. At any rate I'm prepared to go if everything works out," then words again failed him, and he found his eyes again searching hers out, then forced them to look at the top of her head, taking in the quiet tint of red and gold, then gazing foolishly on the wall behind her.

She caught his gaze, began to turn and follow his eyes, when she realized that there was only a blank wall behind her. She gave an involuntary giggle that brought his eyes back to her, then he too broke into a grin, slightly crooked, and finally they both laughed.

This had all taken but a moment, and it seemed lost on Ruth, who pulled him off to meet someone else, a wasted effort as far as he was concerned. All that he saw was a pair of hazel eyes with gold flecks in them, and soft red and gold hair that in his imagination could only be a halo.

It was sometime later that he found himself sitting beside Peter. Almost nonchalantly he said: "Where is Miss Donnell going to work? Anywhere near your station?"

Peter turned a quizzical and humorous eye on his friend. Softly he said as though to himself: "Not the old bachelor? Not the confirmed bachelor? Not the Prof . . . ?" over and over until the latter pounded his shoulder, then laughed with embarrassment.

"Look Peter, you've got to admit that she is not exactly a picture of what is usually considered the missionary type. Not from the cartoons anyway. And besides, I'm just curious. . . ."

"Of course, of course," the other man was totally unsympathetic to the tone of appeal. "But Pat has that effect on people. I'll set your mind at rest. She is a confirmed spinster, and feels that the work to which she has given her life must come first. Apart from that, she is one of the most wonderful women I have ever met — apart from Ruth, of course," and his eyes sought out his wife at the other side of the room. "And for your information, she graduated this year from Bible college, is also a graduate nurse, not a teacher," and his eyes mocked the man who swung around on him, "so you will have nothing in common." And he went on slowly and teasingly, "It is most likely that she will be stationed about 50 miles from where we will be. She will supervise a bush clinic that Bill McAdams hopes to open. Any more questions?" and he looked fondly at his friend.

"No thanks," replied the other. "I'm glad to get off so lightly. No more questions." And all the while, deep inside, he heard the question until it hurt: "Is it? Can it really be? Can it really be?" His question had no answer.

Thirteen

The days that followed Michael
Woods' decision were full. He spent as much time as possible
with the Dunnings, and several times he met Pat Donnell there.
It wasn't until much later that he learned that, woman-like, Ruth
had made these meetings possible.

And as the two shared experiences and the new situations
in which they found themselves, they seemed to draw closer and
closer together.

For the Prof, it was an entirely new experience. For years
he had lived alone and with his work; in more recent years he
had been interested in teaching mainly to help support the
mission work of Peter and Bill. Women had played a very
minor part in his life, and his social contacts with them had been
held to the minimum. Now he found himself in a strange en-
vironment, and a delightful one.

Intellectually brilliant himself, he enjoyed the quiet, common sense of this girl who could talk so easily of his own field
of science, deal with the world problems that were so often dis-
cussed in this global-conscious home, and yet underneath he
felt the constant hard core of someone set in purpose that ex-
cluded the flippant effeminacy that he had grown so used to,
and for which he cared so little.

And day by day, the two fell deeper in love.

It was not something spectacular. It was that quiet satisfaction with each other's company, the silences that spoke
volumes, the sense of completeness as they planned a new life
in Africa. And more and more they seemed to see that new life
as one together.

Michael first gave voice to his feelings. "Pat," they were
sitting in the Dunnings' living room and the host and hostess
had discreetly gone out to the kitchen to prepare a snack. "Pat,
I don't know how to say it nicely, nor do I have any experience
in speaking romantically. But it would seem as though God had
spoken to us at the same time to serve Him; He had led us to

the same mission and the same work. Do you think . . . ?" he paused as though groping for words that came hard to him. The girl turned to the man, a soft light in her eyes.

"Mike," and her whispered tone was almost a caress, "no one has even come near to interesting me before, not since I trusted in Christ as my Saviour. But this is true: my work must always come first. Let's be good friends. Then if He continues to lead us, and we both feel the same when we get to Africa . . . then . . ." she left the sentence unfinished.

Mike gave what was almost a sigh of relief. "You know, Pat," and he picked up her hand and held it lightly, "that has given me the most wonderful sense of relief and release. I guess I should go to school again and learn how to say the right things. . . ."

"You say the right and the nice things," Pat interrupted him.

"Well, I'm about ten years older than you are, and I feel like a small boy beside you. But Pat," and he held her hand tightly, "all these years I must have been waiting for someone just like you. I can wait longer, but I want you to know this: I love you. I have never loved or wanted a woman before, but I love you, and want you to know it. Someday I may have a greater right to say it to you, but tuck it in your heart and know that I love you, and I doubt if anyone has ever been loved so before." He chuckled. "You know, I suppose every man feels that way, and I guess the poets have written about it. But it sounds new, original, and wonderful to me as I say it," and he grinned his boyish grin.

"And to me," she said softly, then pulling her hand away from him, she fled to the refuge of the kitchen and her friends.

Mike followed slowly, a new lightness and joy in his heart.

It was a week later that Peter knocked on the teacher's door, and when it was opened, he entered the room slowly, his face a mask. Woods looked up quickly at his friend, then fear suddenly clutching his heart and squeezing it tightly, he said: "Peter, what is it? Has anything happened to Pat . . . ?" the words seemed to spill out of his mouth.

Peter could only shake his head. He seemed too full to speak for a moment. Then getting a grip on himself, he laid a hand on the arm of his friend and led him over to the fireplace where they had stood and planned a new life some short weeks before. What a picture they had painted then in their minds.

Standing in front of the fireplace, Peter turned to his friend and, in a strangled voice, he said: "No, Mike, it isn't Pat." Then he paused, and finally, in a nearly normal voice he began.

"You remember the full medical you had two weeks ago?" His friend nodded. "The reports came back today, together with your x-rays and tests. Mike," and with a heart full of compassion, he again laid his hand on his friend's arm. "The doctor called and asked me if he should tell you or if I should. I asked him to let me come and do it. Mike," again that choked feeling that almost cut the words off, "your x-rays show a definite shadow in the right lung, what he called a solitary lesion in the right apex," and suddenly the tears welled up in his eyes, and as only a strong man can, he turned his back and wept.

Michael Woods was transfixed for a moment as a realization of what he had heard swept over him. In a moment, Peter had control of himself and turned back to his friend, who still stood, pale and staring. He had just thought of Pat.

The two were men again, and by common consent they sat down in the easy chairs, facing each other. Then slowly and carefully, Peter told all that he knew.

"And the doctor wants you to go in tomorrow for a more complete check, and then you will have to decide what needs to be done.

"Mike," and Peter was clasping and unclasping his hands, "I have been trying to think during the past hour about my share in all this. Did I interfere with the will of God by daring to ask if you would go to the field with us? Was I usurping the work of the Holy Spirit by even suggesting it to you. Then suddenly it came to me: if I hadn't done this, you would not have had a medical for a long time to come, and it might have been too late."

"You're right there, Peter," the teacher said quietly. "I haven't had any kind of a medical since I visited you five years ago in Africa. And I only had it then in order to get a visa."

"Then perhaps the Lord *is* in all this, Mike, and has some wonderful things in store for you." His face brightened. "Mike, tomorrow you will know the truth of your condition. Tonight, before we do know, let us pray about it and ask God to have His own perfect way in everything."

"Thanks, Peter," and the other reached out a hand that trembled slightly. "I don't need anything more than that just now."

The two men knelt, side by side, in that perfect cama-

raderie of an old friendship and the sense of oneness in Christ.
Peter prayed.

"Our heavenly Father . . ." there was this feeling of another
Presence in the room that he always felt when Peter prayed.
A peace began to steal over the teacher. "We want to thank
Thee tonight for the long years of friendship that have been so
constant and true because we know Thee as our true Friend and
One who sticketh closer than a brother. We thank Thee for
the death of Thy Son, for His shed blood, and for His wonderful
resurrection. In all this we see Thy love for us; we see the pro-
vision made for our salvation; we find the new life that is rich,
abundant and eternal, and because He lives, we too shall live."

He paused as though in wonder at the ever new, ever fresh
miracle of the grace of God. Then he continued: "Tonight we
come to Thee as two friends who need Thee as we never have
before. We stand on the threshold of the unknown, and, Father,
we confess to a sense of fear and wonder. Come close to us,
we pray Thee, and lay Thy hand upon Michael Woods, Thy
servant and Thy child. He does love Thee. He has surrendered
his life to Thee. He was ready and willing to follow Thee to
Africa. Father, this is a new way that he didn't expect. Make
him brave and faithful in following Thee here too.

"And Father," Peter's voice broke just for a moment, then he
went on, "Father, I commit to Thee Michael and Pat," he
heard a sharp intake of breath beside him, as though for the
first time the man had realized what this could mean to the
one he loved. Peter heard a barely whispered groan: "Oh God,
and Pat . . ." then silence. After a moment, Peter continued his
prayer: "Father, Mike has come to a tangled mountain. Make
the way clear before him. Make the way plain and open. Help
him to go up, not in pride or his own strength, but in submission,
in devotion, in worship before Thee. Help him to climb up
on his hands and upon his feet. We leave him with Thee. Show
him the way tomorrow. Give the doctor skill and wisdom. And
we look to Thee in an optimism of faith, knowing that Thou
wilt do exceeding abundantly above all we ask or think. Thou
hast promised that 'all things shall work together for good to
those that love Thee, to those who are the called according to
Thy purpose.' He loves Thee, we love Thee. Now make the
good to be known. We ask it all for Jesus' sake. Amen."

He waited for a moment, then slowly rose to his feet. As
he did so, the Prof looked up, smiled as though he had suddenly

found new sources of strength and peace, then he too rose to his feet.

"Would you come and stay with Ruth and me tonight?" asked the thoughtful Peter.

"Thanks, Peter, you are a true friend. But I think I can live with it tonight. Particularly after that prayer. Say good night to Ruth for me — and Peter, it is in God's hands."

Together they walked to the door, another handclasp that was strong and firm, then Michael Woods was alone. He leaned against the door, a great sigh rent from the depths of his chest. The battle had really begun.

Fourteen

Michael Woods left school early the next day to keep his appointment with the doctor. And as he made his way through the corridor that led to his office, he seemed to be walking in a world of unreality, as though it were someone else and he was standing on the sidelines watching.

The smell peculiar to medical offices assailed his nose. It was that peculiar combination of laundry water and ether smell that he loathed, and he wondered how anyone could stand it day after day. "Get used to it, I suppose," he muttered to himself. "Perhaps the smell of the school would get these people down the same way."

He made his way to the office, where he saw the doctor's name in gold and black letters on the frosted glass of the door. Turning the handle, he entered and found himself in a large waiting room with leather-covered chairs scattered around the wall. Most of them were already occupied, and he made his way over near a somewhat noisy air-conditioning unit and settled into the shiny smooth seat of a chair. Idly he looked around. Some of the people were thumbing through the dog-eared magazines, unseeing eyes scanning page after page, but without the look of real interest. Others sat, almost somnolent and apathetic, each one lost in the depths of his own thoughts.

Wonder what would happen if I casually mentioned that I thought I had cancer of the lung, Mike thought as he looked around. Suddenly it hit him with the force of a blow. It was the first time he had even mentioned the possibility to himself. *Cancer. . . .* What a dreadful sound it had. It sounded so — so — so final.

He heard his name mentioned and looked up. The receptionist was standing before him.

"Mr. Woods?" the question came from a calmly smiling face. As he nodded she went on: "Dr. Brand will be with you very shortly." And as again he nodded, she gave him another smile and turned back to her little alcove with the tiny desk.

It seemed a long time before he heard his name again, and he got up and followed the receptionist. She opened another door, let him pass in front of her, then closed it again. A genial giant of a man got out of a swivel chair and came over.

"Glad to see you again, Mr. Woods, or may I call you Mike?"

"Please do," replied the other.

"And I'm Don," the massive man put out his hand, a ham-like and solid hand which easily engulfed that of the teacher. "Peter Dunning has talked so much about you, although he calls you 'Prof' most of the time," and his face broke into a great grin, "that I felt I knew you long before you came in for your tests a couple of weeks ago. Great fellow, that Dunning," he added, apropos of nothing.

"He certainly is," the Prof broke in eagerly, "one of the best. Did you ever meet Bill McAdams — Dr. McAdams who works with him in Africa?"

The other chuckled. "I sure did. Bill and I played water polo together at Varsity. He had a wicked back hook that could take a man's head off if he wasn't ready for it. I'm thankful I always played *with* him and not against him," and he rubbed his unruly thatch of hair. "McAdams is the best. I saw a little of him when he was home on furlough, and must say that from all I heard from him, he is really living. Sometimes I'd like to get out of this rat race too — but that's another story. Let's take a look at yours."

He turned to a big brown envelope that was lying on his desk, and out of it he drew some large x-ray negatives. Flicking a switch that illuminated a frosted panel, he put the negatives one by one into a clip at the top of the glass, took a quick glance, then pulled them down. Mike watched with interest.

After about six of them had gone up and been pulled down, he put in another, then dropped the remainder in his hand and leaned forward. Woods saw what was evidently an x-ray of his chest, the elliptical ribs standing out stark and clear in the misty area. The doctor was peering intently at the picture, then he turned to the patient. He was very matter of fact and casual as he said: "Here, Mike," and as the other stood at his side, he pointed with a huge finger to an area on the right of the center line. As he did so, Mike saw, somewhat imperceptibly, a ragged shadow, about the size of an egg. The doctor's finger traced the rough outline of the shadow, then he switched off the light and turned in his chair.

"Can I talk to you straight, Mike?" he asked abruptly.

"That's the way I want it, Don," replied the other. "A lot hinges on what you tell me, and I want the truth."

"Fine." The doctor got up, moving his great hulk with an ease that surprised the teacher. He took a step or two away from the desk and then came back. "I'll have to make a couple more tests on you," he said finally, "but it looks as though there is some trouble in the right lung, or perhaps just outside of it. It could be malignant or it could be benign." Then as the other looked up hopefully, he went on: "I know, everyone thinks of a growth in the lung as lung cancer. Sometimes it is, sometimes it isn't. There is another condition called 'sarcoidosis' that is benign, and while it can cause some discomfort, it can also be treated fairly easily and rarely calls for more serious probing than a biopsy — a test that we make to see if it is malignant," he explained, when he saw the questioning look on the face of his patient.

"If it is malignant, there is every hope that you have been caught in time and we can get it out. It will mean a lobectomy. Either way, it is going to mean some time in the hospital, first for the biopsy, and then for surgery if it is indicated. Time is of the essence. Can you get into the hospital as soon as I can arrange for a bed?"

"I'm in your hands, Don," replied the other, feeling the beads of sweat that were beginning to form on his forehead. "I'll confess that I'm shaky about the business, but I'm in your hands. And they seem capable of holding me," and he grinned as he looked at those massive members that were toying idly with the envelope the x-rays had come in.

The other looked down, then lifting one enormous paw, he flexed it slowly, the fingers supple and strong. "'We are fearfully and wonderfully made,'" he quoted. "I often look at these hands and see the most amazing engineering feat of all. I do things with these hands that no man-made equipment could do." The fingers were writhing in and out. "I can pick up the smallest article," and with thumb and forefinger he lifted a pin off a glass tray on the desk. "Or with these same fingers I can. . . ." he leaned over, picked up the large telephone book that was lying on a table, and with the utmost ease, he tore it in two as though it were a single sheet of paper. The teacher looked at him in utter amazement.

"I never use a phone book, and I've been looking for an excuse to get rid of it," said the doctor with a grin, dropping the two pieces of the book into a waste paper basket. "I'll never know why they even put one in here. I only use the phone here to answer calls that get past my nurse." He paused. " 'Fearfully and wonderfully made,' " he said again. "You know when Bill McAdams was at medical school with me, he took me to the Christian Fellowship group for that faculty, and it was there for the first time that God became real to me. And it was while I was with that terrific bunch of fellows that I found that Jesus Christ was more than an historical character, or the lead actor in a myth presentation." He stopped, looking at his friend almost sheepishly. "I didn't mean to preach, Prof," the name slipped out, "but as a doctor who spends as much time looking inside the human body as I do the outside, I can only say that apart from God, life, the body, this world have no meaning and no reason for being. 'In him we live and move and have our being,' " the great voice was calm and soothing, and Mike began to feel something of a strange peace as he realized that here was a kindred soul, a man of "like precious faith."

"McAdams and Dunning did the same for me," Mike broke in, then briefly told of his first early contacts with the two high school students who had such a strong Christian faith. "And as you know, I was getting ready to throw in my lot with them. Until *this* came along," he couldn't help a note of bitterness creeping into his voice as he swept his hand across his chest.

The doctor was recalled to his work. "Take your shirt off and let me listen to what is going on in there." And while the teacher was removing his shirt, the doctor took his stethoscope out of his pocket and hooked the ends around his neck.

He examined the chest and back thoroughly, tapping with those fingers, now sensitive and soft, feeling rather than hearing, with his head cocked to one side. Then laying the mouth of the stethoscope to the chest, he asked the patient to cough, moving it from spot to spot as he listened. When it was over he was whistling silently through his teeth, just a sibilant swish of air coming out of his mouth.

"Something there all right," he said at last. "More than that I cannot say. But Mike, 'we are fearfully and wonderfully made.' I know that you are trusting God for the future, and so am I. I'll make arrangements as quickly as possible. You had better get several weeks off at school, and then we will notify them if it has to be longer. Okay?"

"Fine, Don. And thanks a lot. You don't know how much better I feel knowing that I have both you and the Great Physician on this case." The doctor linked his arm through the teacher's and together they returned to the waiting room, the one towering over the other. "My nurse will get in touch with you as soon as possible. In the meantime . . . God," and he pointed his great finger upwards. Then swinging his arm down, he turned and went back to his office.

Michael Woods made his way home.

Fifteen

His phone was ringing shrilly as he went into the apartment, and he lunged for it without closing his door. He wanted to hear someone's voice. It was Peter.

"What's the report, Mike?" he asked as soon as the greeting was over.

As simply as he could, he explained what he could remember of the doctor's explanation. Speaking into the impersonal receiver, he again had the peculiar sensation of being a spectator, as though all this was happening to someone else.

"Mike," Peter's voice cut through the conversation, "Ruth has just called me and asked you to come over for dinner. Will you?"

"Well, I confess I don't feel much like eating, but I don't feel like being alone either. So if you can stand me spoiling your evening, I would be tickled to come over."

"Spoil our evening!" the other shouted, "I'll spoil something else. Get over here as fast as you can. We'll water the soup." And the phone clicked.

It was Ruth who met him at the door, a solicitous, tender Ruth. She rose on her tiptoes and kissed him. "Dear Mike," she murmured, "you know how all this is touching us, don't you?" She gave a little choke, recovered her voice and went on, "But both Peter and I are sure of one thing. Whatever this means, God does not make a mistake. We are going to believe that together, aren't we?"

Woods didn't trust himself to speak, and nodded dumbly. Then as Ruth took his arm and pulled him toward the living room, she said: "Go in there for a few minutes. Peter will be along shortly. I'm getting dinner ready," and with a little shove in the small of his back, she urged him into the living room.

The man moved slowly into the quiet room, and as he did, a girl got out of a chair at the far end of the room.

"Pat!" he thought he had shouted the word, but his mouth was so dry that no sound had come out. "Pat, you here?"

She came toward him slowly, an indefinable expression on her face. All her womanhood, the latent motherhood seemed to shine from her eyes as she approached her man. Still moving steadily, she came up to him, put her arms around his neck, and looked firmly into his eyes.

"Mike," never had he heard his name said this way before, "Mike, inside everything is so mixed up since Ruth told me this morning what you are facing. I have been nerving myself to say this: we don't know what the future holds, but we do know Who holds the future. Mike, let us be strong, and show the world what Christ can mean." The beautiful face so close to his sagged a little. "It sounds so easy to say, and deep, deep down I know it is all true. But, oh *Mike.* . . ." all her poise fled, and she was weeping on his breast, great, heart-rending sobs that threatened to tear her.

Woods stood, nerving himself against breaking down himself. Then slowly he raised his hand and laid it gently on that wonderful hair that he loved to see sparkling in the light. "Pat," and with his other hand he lifted her face to make her look at him, "Pat, I fought this until I had no strength left. Last night I cried as I have never cried before. I questioned, I prayed, I pled with God to make it 'not so' . . . and when my fight was over, I learned something of peace and quiet such as I have never known."

His quiet strength seemed to reach her, for soon the tears and mist passed from her eyes and she looked up at the man she had grown to love, and with whom in the secret of her own heart she had planned and dreamed. He went on: "I am not being dramatic nor brave. I just know that all things are going to work together for good — His good — because I love Him — *we* love Him," he corrected himself, smiling faintly, his hand still lying softly on her head, "and we are the called according to His purpose.

"Pat," he went on, "I've never had to prove God very much. Things have come rather easily. Even my planning to go to Africa was an easy thing as far as I was concerned. Perhaps I needed this . . ." his words trailed off.

Pat still had her arms around his neck. Now she began to move back a little, looking up into his face that was almost level with hers. "Thanks, Mike," she whispered in that soft, quiet voice he loved to hear, "thanks. I'll remember. I just want you to know that I will be with you all the way, until the way is seen clearly again." She paused, and as she did, Mike dropped his hand from her head and pulling her closely he said: "Together, Pat and Mike," and he smiled into her eyes. Then quickly and almost reverently, he brushed her lips with a light kiss, felt her fleeting response, then dropped his hands to his side. It was no kiss of passion. It was a seal. Together they turned back into the living room and sat down in front of the fireplace. There was no need for words.

Sixteen

Michael Woods lay on the stretcher, drowsy and quiet, his thoughts far from the hospital scene that was around him. Through his drugged mind were passing weird scenes, strange voices kept intruding, and sometimes he tried to answer.

Then vaguely he felt the motion of the stretcher, the surging motion of an elevator, the sound of far away voices, and an intolerable glare from brilliant lights. A hand raised one eyelid.

"All right, Mike," it was the voice of Dr. Brand, now subdued as he spoke to the man on the stretcher.

Stiffly there came from the dry lips: "Okay, Don, let 'er roll," then blackness swept over the patient, the eye grew dim, then rolled back, and the doctor dropped the eyelid. He turned to the waiting nurse, and with sure, deft movements he began his work.

❖   ❖   ❖   ❖

The fog slowly lifted from his mind and Mike stirred, tried to sit up, then fell back as he felt a hand on his left shoulder. "Please lie quietly, Mr. Woods," said a voice, "lie quietly and you will feel all right. . . ." Then suddenly she grabbed a basin as he retched then threw up violently. Still groggy, the patient tried to apologize, then the dark curtain came down again and he slept. The nurse quietly cleaned up, keeping an eye on her patient all the while.

Mike had received the first report of the biopsy calmly. Malignancy was indicated, and carefully Don Brand had told him exactly what must be done in the lobectomy. He had stayed in the hospital for several days as they prepared him for the ordeal of surgery. Now it was over, and his special nurse was watching carefully as he slowly came out of the anaesthetic. The vomiting was quite natural, and so far the post-operative period seemed to be normal. She sat down again at the side of the bed, close to his head. She must keep him from moving too violently until he was awake enough to control his actions.

78

It was sometime later when the eyes, dull and glazed, opened again. This time there was no vomiting, and carefully she wiped his face, brushing back the damp hair from his forehead.

"Dr. Brand will be in shortly," she said, using the tone reserved for little children. "Just lie quietly; you are doing fine."

He tried to smile, then grimaced as pain shot like a knife through his chest and sweat spurted out on his forehead. This was quickly wiped away, and as the nurse did so, she felt a hand on her elbow. She looked up and saw the doctor. Quickly she moved to one side and let him sit down near the patient's head.

"Hi, Mike." The deep voice was again under complete control for the sick room. "Feel okay?"

"Okay, Don, let 'er roll," the last words he had uttered before the operation rolled out of his subconscious again. "Fine thanks," he muttered painfully.

"Mike, if you can understand me clearly, wink your eye," said the doctor, speaking carefully. He watched, and saw the flicker of the eyelid. "Fine. I just want you to know that we got everything out, and there should be no further trouble. It is good we found it so early. It was just beginning," and the good doctor's face was beaming.

The words and their meaning slowly penetrated the fogged mind of the patient. Then the therapy of good news brought a strange look of peace to his face and again he slept.

The doctor waited a few moments, then slowly got up, gave a few whispered instructions to the nurse, and left the room. As he did so three figures rose from chairs in the waiting room and went to him.

"Don, how is he?" Almost breathlessly, Ruth was asking the question. The other two did not need to speak. Their faces were gazing hungrily at the doctor, as though they would pull words out of him.

"Well," he said, putting a professional look on his broad face and letting his massive hand stroke his chin. "I should rightly say as well as can be expected," then noticing that he did not bring a like response from the three, he dropped the pose.

"Sorry folks, I guess this isn't the time to joke. But really, he is fine as far as I can see. The operation was amazingly successful, and I'm positive we got everything out. It will take him some months to get back on his feet though, then a long convalescence after that. But he should be as good as ever, considering that he will be missing that piece of his lung." Then in quick terms he told them what he had done. The three waited in silence.

It was Peter who asked the next question that all three had on their hearts.

"What about Africa, Don?" he asked quietly, but with an undercurrent of anxiety that he couldn't hide.

The doctor gave a start. "You know I had completely forgotten what it was that I first examined him for. Africa, of course," and he snapped his fingers so that they went off like a pistol shot. He chewed for a moment on one finger, and Peter, who knew him so well, noticed the sign of perturbation.

"I'm sorry, of course, but Africa is out. Utterly impossible, and I would never be responsible for leaving even a shred of hope that he could ever go there, even for a visit. I could be wrong," and he shrugged his shoulders, "but from my knowledge of cases like this, he can live a perfectly normal life here. I wouldn't guarantee a thing in a country like Africa with heat and humidity so intense and for such long periods of time. I'm sorry," and he looked from one to the other in turn. He noticed the flush on the face of Pat Donnell, and suddenly there came the realization of her part in this drama. He could have bitten off his tongue for the quick decision, then realized that he would have had to say it under any circumstances. He had become almost inured to bearing news that was difficult and hard.

The four talked again for a few moments, then assured that they could see Michael in the next day or so, depending on his post-operative condition, they left.

Ruth had her arm through Pat's, and it was fortunate that she did. The girl seemed to be sleep-walking and would have stumbled but for the restraining hand of the other. In silence they reached Dunning's car and climbed in.

"Like to come home with us, Pat?" Peter asked quietly.

Dumbly she nodded her head. There were no words to speak. Slowly the car was put into gear and driven out of the hospital parking lot. Left behind were dreams and plans.

Seventeen

In Africa, they were strange days for Jane. Learning the language, cooking meals, learning how to filter water, gritting her teeth while she chopped off a chicken's head, finding half a dozen pair of eyes following her wherever she went and whatever she did . . . and with it all, little Biriskilla at her heels The time passed with fascinatiing speed.

Of Bill she saw little, except at mealtime, and often that was late. The hospital had been opened the day that they arrived, and a constant stream of patients kept him and his trained dispensers continually on the go, meeting each case and problem with a poise that belied the pressure and inconvenience under which they were working.

Again it was Baru who served as the mentor for the new missionary. As he had taken Peter Dunning under his wing, and then Dr. McAdams, so now he stepped in to initiate the young wife into the mysteries of his Africa.

He taught her how to walk through the long grass, eyes ever on the alert for the deadly viper that haunted the land, day and night. Particularly at night. He took her into the village close by, showed her how to greet his people, what to say and, perhaps more important, what not to say. He found her an apt pupil, her keen musical ear with its gift of perfect pitch able to follow the tonal quality of the language and to reproduce it with an exactness that brought constant murmurs of delight from her hearers. So far, short sentences and isolated words made up her vocabulary, but slowly she began to hear the distinct sounds and then the words that meant the opening of a new world to her.

Jane became fascinated with her African sisters and went as often as she could to the spotless home of Baru's wife, where she was ever welcome. And little Biriskilla was her constant companion, often going beyond Baru's temerity in correcting the language of her white "Mother."

It was on one of these trips into the heart of the village that brought Jane an experience that was to delight her heart beyond the telling. While chatting in her hesitant Hausa, she was conscious of a peculiarly resonant sound that came on the slight breeze blowing through the valley. There was a rhythm and quality about it that tantalized her. Finally she turned to Biriskilla and asked,

"What is that sound I hear?"

The little girl was attentive for a moment, her ear turned in the direction indicated, her flat nostrils flared wide with the intensity of her listening. Then she broke into a grin. *"Dilali ke nan,"* she said in the limpid language of children. "It is Dilali." Seeing that her friend was none the wiser, she reached out a small hand and, saying good-by to the African hostess, she pulled Jane along a narrow path that led between some of the small compounds.

As they walked, the sound became clearer, and Jane noted the music — for such it happened to be — the peculiar melody ringing out on the still air. Her ear caught the first five notes of the scale, but the rest was a combination of the sixth and seventh. She tried to follow it as she walked closer and closer. Then they saw the musician.

Standing under a baobab tree was a slim young African, dressed in white cotton shorts and shirt, his hands pumping up and down rhythmically on an instrument that seemed to be attached to his shoulders. Fearful of having the music stop, Jane put a restraining hand on Biriskilla's shoulder, then stopped, as she stared in amazement.

What she had thought at first to be a table was a portable xylophone, but one such as she had never seen before. About a dozen short ebony rods were laid side by side and held in place by thin, strong grass rope. Almost, but not quite, touching the ends of these rods, were a like number of cows' horns, and the music seemed to be coming from the ends of these. Two ropes suspended the contraption to the shoulders of the young man, leaving his hands free to play the instrument. In each hand was a soft-headed wooden mallet, and with these he was tapping out his music, now slow and plodding, then racing so fast that Jane could scarcely follow the hammers in his hands.

Suddenly a yellow, ribbed dog raced out of a nearby hut, yapping furiously at the strangers. The musician was distracted and turned to see what the disturbance was, only to be confronted with the white woman and her small African friend.

"*Sannu, Dilali,*" said the latter, "*kana lafiya?* Hello, Dilali, are you well?"

"*Ai, sannu, Biriskilla,*" he replied, "I am well. Do you come in health?"

Then the two Africans proceeded with the proper salutations, the tribal code strict even with the stranger in their midst.

When they had finished, Biriskilla introduced her friend: "This is the wife of our doctor," she said, "and she has come to hear your music."

Dilali turned to Jane, and with the extreme politeness of his people, he again went through the salutation ritual, sometimes faster than the missionary could follow, but she replied as the custom was. When they were finished, Jane pointed to his instrument.

"May I look at your *molo?*" Early she had learned the word for a musical instrument. At his nodded assent, she went toward him and looked closely at it. What she had seen from a short distance now showed itself to be a delicately made and beautifully balanced instrument. The short ebony rods were concave on the underside, beautifully polished, and as resonant as fine crystal when she tapped one with her fingernail. She noticed how the hollows on the underside of the bars were of different lengths, each one almost perfectly pitched to complete the six notes of the African scale. She looked carefully at the cows' horns, and saw how they had been hollowed out until they were paper thin, almost transparent. At the top or pointed end of the horn was some black gummy substance, and as she peered closely she noted that it covered about half of the small opening. The rest of the opening was covered by a thin gauze-like material; the gum was there only to hold it in place. Later she learned that this was a single layer from a spider's nest that one could find in corners or crevices of the mud walls of the houses of the people.

Taking one of the small hammers, she saw that it was a very soft, fibrous wood. The knobbed head had been scored and cut until it was a mass of small slivers bound to the handle. Tentatively she tapped one of the rods. Crystal clear, the single note rose slowly from the instrument, like a bubble of released air in rich, red wine. She tapped another, registering the notes on her ear as she did so. Then the whole scale with its six notes lay before her mind's eye, and with an impish grin, she tapped out the very tune that the African had been playing.

Biriskilla jumped around and around her, clapping her hands in childish glee, while Dilali stood there, his mouth and eyes both wide open.

"*Mai Molo, Mai Molo,*" he repeated over and over again. "Your name is *Mai Molo,* the Musician." And that day, Jane received the name that was to be hers for the rest of her African days.

The two were almost oblivious to the people who were beginning to gather around. Jane had found what she had never expected to find in Africa . . . a kindred musical soul. And Dilali was fascinated at the quick skill of this slim young white woman, playing his instrument in a way that he had thought possible only for him.

Finally he slipped the ropes from his shoulders and indicated that Jane should put them on her own. She slipped her arms through the two loops, felt the instrument settled against her abdomen, then with a hammer in each hand, she began to tap out, in limpid pure notes, some of the simple melodies that she had heard the people sing in the mission church and around their own fires.

Heat, dirt, and strange surroundings were gone. Music was here, and the girl reveled in it. As her hands became more skilled, so her music became more intricate. Occasionally she would suck in her lip in her characteristic habit when concentrating, as she sought to bridge the gap of the note missing on her instrument. But none of her fascinated audience would have criticized her. And she played on and on.

Finally heat and exhaustion from the unaccustomed arm work slowed the music, and Jane looked up from the instrument. Her eyes widened. Packed around the tree was a dense mass of people, eyes shining, white teeth glistening out of the surrounding area of black skin. She never had a more appreciative audience.

Africans do not clap their hands, but if there is the equivalent in words, verbal hands were clapped. Jane slipped the ropes off her aching shoulders and handed the instrument back to Dilali.

"Thank you, Dilali. Bring this to the mission house sometime. I would like to hear you play it, and to play it myself."

Dilali took the xylophone from her hands. He seemed dazed. Then he looked at her and admiration shone in his face.

"No one, not even I, has been able to play as you did today, *Mai Molo*. Indeed I will come, for I would hear you play some more. Thank you, thank you," and the African beamed his pleasure.

Jane spoke to Biriskilla, and they quickly made their way through the throng. Taking again the narrow path between the compounds, they hurried home. Jane's feet scarcely touched the ground. She had found music in Africa.

Eighteen

Bill held the letter in his hand. Then calling for Jane, he began running toward the mission house, scarcely able to wait to share the good news with her.

His calling brought Jane to the screen door. "Well, Mr. Man," she asked, "what is all the excitement about?"

"Jane, I have just heard from Peter. A nurse by the name of Pat Donnell—" he stopped suddenly. Then he went on slowly, "is flying out here and should be in Jos next week. This letter must have been held up somewhere. It is nearly four weeks since Peter wrote." Then he looked up at his wife.

"Does the name Pat Donnell ring a bell with you?"

"Pat D— of course, Bill. That's the girl that Mike was so interested in. Peter and Ruth wrote about them. Oh—" and suddenly the realization of what it meant swept over her.

"Oh, Bill, those poor people. No, not poor," she corrected herself, "but I do feel so sorry the way things turned out. I suppose after Mike's lobectomy they faced this thing, and she is coming out here alone. Bill," she turned brimming eyes to him, "that is exactly what you were going to do, isn't it, when I was so stubborn and hard. I guess you know something of what Mike feels now. And perhaps I know something of what Pat feels too. The Lord has been so good to us," and she put her arm lovingly through that of her husband and drew him into the cool house. "Come on in and read the rest of Peter's letter."

She sat on the arm of the chair and listened as Bill read the entire letter. Pat would be arriving in Jos by air early the next week, and would Bill please meet her and drive her out to the station? "Here is the nurse we have been praying about for so long," the letter said, "so give her a good introduction to the country. I'm sure that Jane will be glad to have another woman on the station, with you away so much.

"And Bill," the letter went on, "it is impossible for us to get back as soon as we planned. So perhaps you can fix our place up for Pat and she should be very comfortable. Then when

86

I get back we can plan a small place for her to live in. All for now," he had scrawled in the cramped space left, "I will write you a longer letter later, giving you all the news." Then he had scribbled his slanting "Peter" to the letter.

Jane was sitting with her hands in her lap. "I'll get working right away on the Dunnings' place," she said. "Will you go in for her?"

"We'll both go in," he replied, placing his arm around her waist. "You haven't really been off the station or away from the village since you arrived, and it will do you good. Besides, you can help her feel at home right away," and he grinned up at his wife.

"For your information, I have been quite happy here, Mr. Man," she said, pushing her long finger against his nose and squashing it down on his upper lip. "But I will be glad to go into Jos with you, since there are some things I would like to get, now that we are having company," and she got up to plan for the guest who was to come.

"The eternal female," muttered Bill as he watched her put on her sun glasses and go out. "The Dunnings won't know their place when she gets through fixing it up for Pat." As the name flashed through his mind, he thought again of his own battle about Jane, and his heart bled for his old teacher friend, and for this as yet unknown girl whom he had loved. With a sigh, he got up, and taking the same path Jane had taken, headed for the hospital. And as he passed the Dunnings' whitewashed house, he heard Jane talking to Biriskilla in her halting Hausa. He grinned, then passed out of ear-shot, his mind on the work ahead.

Nineteen

Jane fingered the handle on her tea cup idly, her eyes drawn to the other woman in the room. It was only her profile, but Jane could follow the line of the beautifully molded face, with its high cheek bones, the straight nose, and the slightly full lips bright with their own color. She noticed the hair, the little gold flecks seemed to dance and shimmer under the light of the pressure lamp.

"Some more tea, Pat?" She asked the question to break the silence.

The other girl turned, then flushed as she realized that she had been silent so long. "I'm sorry," and Jane heard the lovely tone of her voice, its whisper-like quality blending perfectly with the tropical night. "I'm sorry, I didn't mean to be rude. It just seems that the silence speaks out here, and I was enjoying it."

"I know just what you mean," replied Jane. "The first few days out here, I seemed to hear voices and music in everything. Now I know that some of them are just plain noises," and she laughed gaily.

Pat joined in. The silence broken, the two drew their chairs closer together and began to talk. They were interrupted by the entrance of Bill.

"Tea, tea!" he cried out in mock agony, "tea; my throat is like a lime kiln. Tea, tea, tea," and he let his voice die away as he sagged into the nearest chair.

The girls laughed, then solicitously they both began to prepare his tea. As Jane held his head, Pat put the cup to his lips and let him sip it. He revived quickly. Taking the cup, he gulped down the hot liquid, then mutely held it out for a refill. His wife obliged, and then:

"Why the heroics, Mr. Man?" she asked as she handed him the refilled cup. "You always put on an act when you are planning to tell us something. So out with the news, or you won't get your third cup."

"Never that," he cried plaintively, "I'll give you the news —

when I get my third cup," and so saying he drained the one in his hand and handed it back once more.

With the refilled cup in his hand, he leaned forward, his eyes dancing. "Guess what? Baru and I are heading south the day after tomorrow, and we are hoping to get beyond Bima in two or three days," and he sat back with a satisfied smirk.

"*Bima?*" Jane almost breathed the word. "You mean the tangled mountain?"

"I mean the tangled mountain," he said. "Baru has just met up with a trader who says he knows an easy way across, and he leaves the day after tomorrow, and I leave with him — that is, if you agree," he added hastily.

Jane knew better than to try to dissuade this man of hers. His search for adventure in this wonderful country of Africa was one of the things she admired most about him. But she couldn't help feeling a qualm of fear.

"Is it safe, Bill?" she asked.

"As safe as the Kitta country ever was," he replied, his eyes dancing. "And that was safe except for that leopard episode," and he flexed the arm that had been torn by the leopard's claws.

"Besides," he went on, "it will only be for a couple of days. I want to see what it is like, and what the people are like. What I want to do is see if we can set up an outpost there. If we can, then perhaps Peter and I can alternate down there and do some work for the Lord among the people. Baru says that no one has ever gone there to preach the Gospel, and it is a wonderful opportunity for us. If we can only get across," and he fell to musing, "the one path I know about is impossible for a horse, and I'd like to ride over."

Pat was silent all the while that they were talking. Then she said: "Do you think we could set up a medical clinic there, Bill?" she was almost eager.

"I don't know yet. We always do some medical work. But a clinic. . . ." Then he looked at her with new eyes. "You mean you would like to go there and have a clinic among the people?"

"If it is possible," she nodded eagerly. "It is wonderful being here and helping you, but if we can multiply ourselves this way. . . . And if the Dunnings are there part of the time, and you and Jane part of the time, it should be safe enough for me."

"Poof," said Bill, "I wasn't worrying about safety. You girls are safer here than you would be in your own city at home. It's just — oh language, travel, transporting goods and all that.

However, I'll know better after I have been down there. I'll have to leave the work here in your hands, but there is nothing you can't handle. You've had a month to work into the routine, and it shouldn't be hard."

"Oh, I'll love it," replied Pat enthusiastically. "I've felt so useless trying to learn Hausa and everything else, and doing so little work. But I'll move in here with Jane and we'll look after things until you get back. Just remember, I have squatter's rights to a clinic over there," and she nodded her head to the south.

"Yours it is," replied Bill gallantly, then he began talking over the work that would be in their care until he returned. And all the while, the little bubble of excitement that always gripped him when he was planning a new move threatened to draw his attention away from the work at hand. He resolutely put the thoughts of the journey out of his mind.

"Here is a list of the patients in the ward now . . ." and he began giving directions for the work to be done in his absence. And as he spoke, Pat was writing down his instructions.

Occasionally Bill shot a quick look at the girl. Shortly after her arrival, she had unburdened herself to Jane about Mike and his lobectomy and the crash of their dreams. But never once had she indicated anything but complete satisfaction over the step she had taken. No anodyne was needed here. The perfect peace of surrender had kept and would keep this girl. Bill looked at her in admiration.

Once, on looking up from her writing, she saw his eyes on her. Quickly a smile lit up her face.

"A question, Doc?" she mocked his look.

"Well, yes," he replied, unruffled. "Why are you so anxious to go to Bima — or do you know its story?"

"Peter Dunning told us about the tangled mountain the night I dedicated my life for missionary service," she replied quietly, "and ever since I arrived, I have wanted to see it. Besides it has a little more meaning to me." She paused reflecting. "When Peter spoke of it, he was using an illustration of difficult places in our lives. I had one, as you know," and he nodded. There was no need to mention Michael Woods. "The Lord helped me get beyond that tangled mountain — so I would like to get beyond this physical one too. It means a lot to me," she added impulsively.

"As soon as we can work it, you'll be there," said Bill emphatically. Then he returned to the hospital report and Pat started writing again.

Twenty

The sun was sending its bands of gold and purple over the ridge of the hill behind the mission house when Bill swung into the saddle to the nervous side-stepping of his horse. Wisps of mist were rising from the ground, and over the village about a quarter of a mile away it mixed with the smoke of the early morning fires, to lie like a pall over the whole scene.

Sitting at ease in the saddle, Bill looked toward the village, with its closely set collection of huts, each with its tuft of grass pointing up from the center of the thatched roof. As yet, few of the people were out in the hated, early morning cool air. The quiet and the scene always reminded Bill of an ancient woodcut that used to grace the books of adventure and travel before the days of photography.

He loosened the strap on his helmet and swung it to his shoulder. Then, laying the reins gently on the horse's neck, with the slight side pressure that he had trained it to obey, he swung around in a tight circle and cantered back toward the mission house.

Here Jane and Pat, both looking bleary-eyed in the early light, were waiting for him. Jane had her hair done up in a kerchief . . . he had always joked about her being more like a porcupine when her hair was pinned up, until she had vowed he would never see it uncovered. Pat's hair, with its natural wave, needed nothing more than a comb to set it springing and dancing in the early light.

He reined up in front of them and swung down from the saddle, the reins lying loosely in his hands.

"I'm off, girls," and the boy in the man peeped out behind the attempt to hide his satisfaction. " 'How I brought the good news from Ghent to Aix,' " and he grinned a boyish grin.

" 'From Ghent to aches' is more like it," punned Pat, then ducked as he swung the reins at her head.

"Do be careful, Mr. Man," Jane was looking up at him, her love in her eyes. This was to be their first separation since their marriage, and she wondered what it would be like to be alone on the station. Then she remembered Pat, and put her arm around her. "We'll keep the home fires burning. Just come back in one piece." She put her face up to receive his good-by kiss.

"Bye, Jane." He brushed her lips lightly with his, then: "Take good care of her, Pat," and with a wave of his hand he was back in the saddle, set the horse to a mile-eating canter, and flicked off down the mission path, through the cactus hedge, and then was only a bared head, bobbing easily along the road that led down into the valley where he was to meet Baru and the trader for the journey south.

The horse felt the mood of the morning and soon stretched his legs out into a gallop that set Bill crooning with delight. The early morning air whistled past his ears and only the rhythmic clop-clop of the unshod hooves broke the stillness, until he came near the edge of the town. Then there was the wild cacophony of dogs, racing out to bark ferociously at the flying hooves, the roosters setting up their claim on the new day, and finally as he neared the huts, the calls and shouts of children and friends who rolled off their mud or cornstalk beds at the heralding of the rider.

The gallop slowed to a canter and then reined in to a walk as Bill guided the horse through the narrow paths that led to Baru's compound.

He did not need to make known his arrival. A group of the Baru family were gathered in front of a hut, in the center of which was the stubby form of Baru, clearly giving the children their orders for the time he would be away. As Bill rode up, he was talking to Biriskilla.

"You must go and stay on the mission compound with the *uwargida Mai Molo.*" He was waving his hand in that direction when his eyes saw the doctor coming along the path.

Turning, he greeted his friend, the lengthy salutations losing none of their meaning for their repetition. A warm bond had sprung up between these two whose cultures were so far removed but whose hearts and lives were so entwined. The one did not see a white man, but a friend, a brother for whom he would, and once nearly had, died. The other did not see an African, a black man. For this missionary was one who was "color blind" and what he saw was a brother in Christ, a close friend and confidant, a good companion whose bubbling sense of humor ("sensayumer" as Bill always mentally said it) made light the African miles they had traveled together.

"Here we go again, Baru," was Bill's comment after the salutations were finished.

"We catch the road again, *Likita*," replied the other, a grin of anticipation splitting his face. "It has been a long time. Now we two are one again," and he turned back to finish his instructions. Bill waited patiently, still on his horse.

Baru finished talking to Biriskilla, who needed no other encouragement but turned back into the square, adobe-type house that Baru had built, rolled up a sleeping mat and gathered her few belongings to take with her to the mission station. Not often was she permitted this luxury, and there would not be a minute wasted.

His instructions finished, Baru let out a call that was almost a whoop, and shortly his oldest son appeared, leading two dun-colored horses. On seeing Bill's eyebrows raised, Baru explained.

"When the chief heard where we were going, he insisted on loaning horses to us, one for me and one for Amadu."

"Amadu?" asked McAdams.

"The trader I told you about," replied Baru. "He says that he knows a way over the Bima that we can ride, and I thought we might be able to travel faster that way." He paused as a man came out of his hut, his eyes blinking in the early light.

He was a tall, light skinned African, thin of face and aquiline of nose. There was an Egyptian or Jewish cast of feature that Bill tried to recall. Then he remembered. The man must be a Fulani.

"*Walli jam.*" The Fulani greeting sprang unbidden from Bill's lips, the action to the thought that had raced through his mind as he had identified the man.

The stranger looked startled, the jerk of his head almost sending the loosely bound turban to the ground. "*Walli jam,*" he replied, "*jam.*" Then turning to Baru, he said in Hausa, "Your friend speaks Fulatanci?"

Baru was grinning like a cheshire cat. "Speak to him a little more in your tongue," he replied, "and you will see."

The stranger turned back to Bill and spoke rapidly, the tones running up and down the scale at a rate that made the missionary's ears take them all in as one rolling sound. The doctor could only grin at the spate of words, entirely unknown to him. Finally he held up his hand. *"Hankali, hankali,"* he said, "take it easy. I used my two Fulani words. I know no more."

Almost disappointed, the man stopped the flow of words, then reverting to Hausa, he gave the usual salutations to the man on the horse. Bill replied in kind, and when the amenities were over, he said:

"We do not often see your people down this way at this time of year. Where are your cattle?"

The man waved a negligent hand toward the south. "My people are following the river with the cattle," he replied. Then his attitude became somewhat furtive, and it was not lost on the missionary. "I am going beyond the Bima to seek new markets for our cattle and butter." The reply was so implausible that Baru jerked around from tying his grass mat on the horse and stared at the man. He said nothing, however, and soon the horses were ready, their meager traveling equipment tied behind the huge native saddles.

The doctor had already sent his two carriers on ahead, and now he looked with envy at these men who could travel so lightly and easily in this tropical country. For himself, he knew that even minimal traveling requirements would involve two or three times as much as these children of the jungle seemed to require. Behind him on his saddle were his water canteens and the small ingenious lunch kit that he had contrived for a saddle-bag. It contained a small metal teapot, tea, sugar, and the sandwiches that Jane had made up for him the night before, plus a few emergency rations that would keep him going for a day or two and small medical kit.

In the capacious pocket of his bush jacket were the essential water-purifying tablets that had been put on the market after the last war. Invented for the use of the armed forces fighting in the tropics, they were a boon to those who traveled through the bush and jungle. The water that was so plentiful could mean death to the unwary traveler, or at the least, painful guinea worms or bilharzia, unless it was boiled first, or purified, as it could be now by these amazing tablets. Gratefully Bill patted the pocket containing them. He could still remember the agonizing thirst that had gripped him on one trip, saved only by the jungle cunning of Baru who had dug a deep hole in a dried creek bed with his hands, until a small trickle of dirty water had seeped in, and they had both drunk from the slowly forming pool at the bottom of the hole. They had, by sheer force of will, stopped themselves from drinking from the many brackish pools they had come across. Now with the magic tablets, any water was rendered fit and harmless, and Bill never traveled any distance without a supply of them.

The African men were soon ready, and they slipped expertly into the high pommeled saddles. As the sharp bits dug into the horses' mouths, they reared and snorted under the cruel pressure. Then with farewell shouts from riders and friends, the three horsemen picked their way back through the paths, out on to the wider road, and soon left the village far behind.

Bill was in his element. With Baru taking the lead, the stranger Amadu next, he brought up the rear, settling more and more into the relaxed position that staved off the fatigue of saddle travel.

They passed groups of men and women heading off into the bush or to the farms for their day of work. Salutations were cut short as the horses cantered by, high tailed as they were reined in to pass the pedestrians. Then the reins were loosened, and they settled to the canter that would eat up the miles but conserve strength.

The sun had risen higher and higher, and now, with it completely clear of the hills, it poured its full orbed rays on the men as they traveled. The silence of the road settled over them. There was no sound save the horses padding in the thick dust of the trail. *This time,* Bill was thinking, *we will get beyond the tangled mountain.*

Twenty-one

Back at the mission station, Jane watched her husband out of sight, then putting her arm around Pat, they went back into the house to have breakfast before beginning the day's work.

Pat had moved her things into the main house, and the two women were soon happily engrossed in talking and eating, satisfied with the company of each other in their isolation.

Breakfast was finished, Pat had gone up to the small hospital to begin her work, and Jane was busily preparing for the first class of the day when Biriskilla burst in upon her.

"*Mai Molo, Mai Molo!*" The words came out in sharp gasps, her eyes big with excitement, her feet twitching and dancing in sheer ecstasy. "*Mai Molo, wani mota yana zuwa.* A great lorry is coming."

Jane dropped her books, and with the little African girl at her heels, ran out the door and up the short path that led to the road that Bill had had built. And sure enough, as she rounded the path from the kitchen, which was separate from the remainder of the mission house, she saw the dust clouds of an approaching truck just beginning the descent from the hill that divided the village into two sections.

She stood waiting, and as she did so, saw another car behind the truck, a station wagon, from whose window a massive arm was waving frantically. Jane's heart was pounding, then suddenly she recognized the owner of the waving arm in the second vehicle.

"Mrs. Wigle!" she breathed, then was running hard, passing the lorry — for which she only had a second glance to see it piled high with massive crates — and was tugging at the door of the car.

"Dearie!" a moist arm was wrapped around her neck and she was being crushed to the bosom of this mammoth woman, her own arms circling her neck.

To her relief she was soon released from the embrace, then held off at arm's length while critical eyes took in her every line.

"This here Africa must agree with you, dearie," came the booming voice that echoed over the compound. "You look better than you did on that there boat."

"Is this ever a surprise!" were the first words that Jane could get out. And as she did so, she felt a tap on her shoulder.

"Remember me," came the quiet voice from behind her, and Jane whirled. In a moment of exuberance she flung her arms around Mr. Wigle, while his wife stood, grinning hugely.

The man gently kissed the girl, then stood back to survey her.

"Yep," he said, a twinkle in his eye, "some chick, and I'm an authority on chickens," he chuckled, and Jane threw back her head and laughed.

"Where's your husband?" he asked after a moment, during which Pat had joined them and been introduced. He looked around idly.

"He just left this morning, and should be back in a couple of weeks or so," replied Jane, then went on to explain his trip across the Bima hills.

The man smacked his hand into his fist. "Couldn't be better," he exclaimed.

At Jane's questioning glance he went on: "All the equipment for the power plant arrived last week," he said by way of explanation, "and we had it shipped up to Jos. I bought this station wagon, and it arrived before the shipment did," and he patted the dusty fender of his car. "In Jos I asked at the mission headquarters about getting the stuff out here, and they came up with the best answer. Garba," he called in the direction of the lorry. At the sound of his voice, a moon-like face peeped out of the lorry cab, and Jane saw Baru's brother grinning impishly at her. Opening the door of the cab, he lowered himself to the ground, his short, bandy legs lessening the look of pride and dignity with which he did so.

"*Ai, sannu, Mai Molo,*" he gave a half bow before her as was the custom of his people. "*Na zo.* I have come," then he began his salutations.

Jane replied in kind in her halting Hausa, then on his inquiring where the doctor and Baru might be, Biriskilla broke in and in a flood of words told her uncle where the other men had gone. Garba's face fell. The mixture of pride in bringing such an important load to the mission, plus his love for the doctor and his brother, had evidently sustained him all the way from Jos. Now they were not here. Then suddenly realizing that with his brother absent he would have to take charge, he drew himself up, then stalked off shouting some commands to sundry men as he did so.

Jane turned back to the Wigles. "I'm sorry that Bill is not here, but perhaps we can get along until he comes back."

"Get along, young woman, get along, you say? We will get along all right. Actually I'm glad he isn't here — "

His wife broke in: "Merle has been like a hen on a hot brick, if I can use one of his trade jokes," and the woman looked fondly at her husband. "He wants to get his hands into something, and I think he has just been holding on until he could get here and start at some work."

Mr. Wigle nodded his head happily. "With Bill away, I'm going to have a field day, and with some half decent help, I'll have all this stuff set up before he gets back," and he waved his hand at the truck, piled high.

While Jane took Mrs. Wigle into the house and Pat went back to the hospital, he called again for Garba and, with gestures, told him that the lorry was to be unloaded. The boy nodded, and the visitor followed the women into the house.

Over a cup of coffee, the Wigles gave Jane a move-by-move description of their wait in Lagos, the arrival of the equipment for the power plant, and the journey inland. Her story, told with the flourishes, the "that theres," the humor that she saw in everything, had Jane helpless with laughter. Mr. Wigle occasionally and quietly injected his own comment, and soon they were quite caught up on the news of each other.

It was into the quiet of this moment that a series of shrieks brought the three of them to their feet, then out the door where they stood transfixed.

Standing behind the lorry was a great stack of equipment, piled without regard to order or convenience, while teetering precariously on the tailgate was a massive crate, just saved from falling by a half a dozen men who supported its weights on heads and shoulders, all the while shouting unintelligibly. Round and round them, back and forth, raced Garba, sweat pouring off him and fear and anxiety showing on his face.

In a glance the newcomer saw what was wrong. Quickly he turned to Jane: "Do you have any heavy planks?" At her nod, the two ran over to a lean-to building beside the kitchen, where he quickly pulled out two massive mahogany planks. Jane called a couple of bystanders over, and soon they had the planks braced under the crate, forming a skidway down which the men were able to ease their burden. It took just a few minutes, but the shouting, the shrieking, and the constant movement of the people made it seem much longer.

Wigle was sweating profusely before it was over, and Jane walked over to him.

"I'm so sorry," she said, indicating his soaked shirt. "I should have remembered that they would not know how to unload heavy crates like that."

"No damage done," he replied with a grin. "But I had better stay here and see about getting the rest of it off before we break something."

"Is there anything I can do?" asked Jane.

"Yes," he replied. "Could you get me about a dozen men who will work with me? I suppose none of them speak English?"

"Not in a way that would be of real help," she said. "But there are several of them who are quite used to working with Bill and Peter, and you can practically signal anything you want. Then if you get stuck, call me, although I won't be too much help either," and she was almost apologetic.

"Good," he answered. "Just get me some good men, and I'll have a couple of weeks' work for them." He went off to supervise the rest of the unloading and the storing of the equipment, while Jane moved off to speak to Biriskilla. That young lady, sharp and eager, with the keenness of her father stamped on her, would know whom to get. The two of them moved out of the range of the shouting that still came from the men unloading the lorry, while Jane told the girl what was wanted.

At the lorry, Mr. Wigle was doing well with hand signals in showing Garba what should be done, and the latter, taking the role of interpreter, translated into Hausa. Soon the lorry was unloaded, and by this time Jane had returned.

"Well, I have the names of ten or twelve men," she informed him. "I'll send word to them to come down as soon as possible. Some of them are here," and she indicated the men who were walking around the mountain of crates, bags of cement, and boxes that seemed to fill the compound. "When do you want them?"

"Now," he replied with a slight shrug. "This is going to take longer than I thought, but if we can get it rigged or nearly ready before Bill gets back, I'll be happy."

Jane called Garba over and haltingly told him what was required. He grinned his wide grin, then moved off to speak to the men who had been named. Soon he was back.

"They want to work with the man with the voice," and he jutted his chin in the expressive African gesture toward Mr. Wigle. "They call him *Mai waka*, the man with the singing voice," and his eyes twinkled.

Jane was delighted, and told Mr. Wigle what the African had said. He chuckled. "I have heard that it doesn't take long to get a name out here," he said. "I'll try to live up to it, although it won't be singing when things get rough and I have to shout at them."

Garba broke into the conversation and Jane listened intently. Her puzzled look gave way to a frown, and Mr. Wigle stepped closer.

"Something wrong?" he asked solicitously.

Jane bit her lip, then decided to tell him. "Garba was just talking about Mrs. Wigle," and she looked up at the husband. "You know these people are nothing if not frank," and she grinned at him. He smiled back, half anticipating something of what she should say.

"The men were saying, according to Garba, that your wife just puffs herself up like that, somewhat the way a frog does when confronted with some danger. When danger is past, they say she can deflate herself," and despite herself, Jane chuckled.

Wigle looked over in the direction of his wife, who was standing in the middle of a group of women, her strong voice cutting through the babble around her. There was only admiration in his gaze.

Jane went on: "Some of the people thought she should be called *Giwa*, which is Hausa for elephant," and again she was embarrassed. "I don't want her to feel insulted," she went on, "but these people have names like that for their own people, and no offense is intended or taken."

"She will love anything they call her," replied the husband. "She has a heart as big as her body, and is as guileless as a child. They won't offend her."

As best she could, Jane interpreted the conversation to Garba, whose face lighted. He had seen the frown on the face of *Mai Molo* and was disconcerted. Now he spoke: "Ask the *Bature*, the whiteman, if we can call her *Mai Jiki*, the owner of the large body?"

Jane translated this for Mr. Wigle, and he nodded. "Sure, anything. Actually I think she would get a kick out of that elephant name. But just let it take its course," he added wisely, "and before long they will call her the great heart or the magnificent one, or whatever they call the kindest person in all the world."

Jane felt the tug of his words as she spoke, his eyes still on his wife at the other side of the compound. What a difference from the first impression of them on board ship when he had seemed so mousy and she so overbearing. *How little one knows what goes on under the surface,* she thought, *and how wrong it is to judge by first appearances.* Dismissing Garba, she walked with Mr. Wigle over toward his wife.

She saw them coming and her voice boomed out: "Well, Merle, I see that you got that there truck unloaded all right. When will the lights be turned on?" and her laughter produced an echo from the women standing around her. They didn't know what had been said, but laughter is a universal language, and these fun loving people loved the chuckle and the boom in this large woman's voice. Jane could almost see the way these people would take her to their hearts, and she in turn would take them to hers, language barrier or no.

Merle looked at her. "Jane got me some men," he replied to her laughing question, "and as soon as I can get into some work clothes and my tools lined up, we set to work."

"Then I work too," she replied, and turned to Jane. "What's first?"

"Well, first is to get you settled," replied the practical Jane. "Do you realize that you have only been here a couple of hours, and we haven't planned where you will stay. Let's get your things up to the Dunnings' house, and start there." Putting her arm through that of her friend, the two moved toward the station wagon to get the bags and cases piled in its back.

Mr. Wigle watched them go, then turned to Garba and began his signals. It was time to work.

The next few days saw the mission station in a whirl of activity that it had never known before. Garba and Mr. Wigle worked together amazingly well for their signal language. Some men were set to mixing cement, while Wigle superintended the making of forms where the great diesel power unit would finally sit and send out its electricity to the hospital and houses.

Wigle was in his element, learning with ridiculous ease short phrases that he used to good effect, watching with admiration the sleek, wiry bodies of the Africans as they worked, listening to their singing, recognizing tunes but not words, and surmising that they were some of the Hausa hymns that followed the time-honored music even in translation.

And day by day, Mrs. Wigle moved closer and closer to the hearts of the people. One day she was at the hospital, crooning over a wee black mite whose swollen abdomen indicated a spleen enlarged through constant malaria. Often she would be seen striding up into the village with Jane and Biriskilla, her loud voice heralding their approach, her quick, eager eyes seeming to take in, in one rapid glance, the people, their homes, and their work. She seemed tireless, and a panting Jane tried to keep up with this human dynamo.

"And to think I could have been out here thirty years ago," was her constant personal rebuke, and off she would go, eagerly seeking to help here, encourage there, and taking all and sundry to the heart that her husband had said would be big enough to take them all in.

Soon Jane heard the people referring to *Mai Taimako*, the helpful one, and the elephant and the frog episode were soon forgotten. A helper she was, to Jane, to Pat, and to the people. Her energy was inexhaustible, and her capacity to love unlimited. It was good to have her on the station.

Her husband too, quietly and efficiently, began to fit into the work, and soon it seemed as though they had always been there. A sense of well being settled over the four and their work, and Jane began to anxiously wait word from Bill regarding his trip and plans. He was all that was needed to make the idyll complete.

Twenty-two

                    Bill was almost dozing, soporific in the heat and with the rocking motion of the horse, now slowed to a lazy walk. Occasionally his hand swept up to dislodge the flies that insisted on clustering on his mouth and eyes, their buzzing the only sound in the broad valley.

Baru was still in the lead and the stranger Amadu second, his loose burnoose catching at branches and bushes on each side of the narrow trail.

At midday Bill called a halt, asking the two men if they knew if there was a stream or well nearby where they could water the horses and refresh themselves.

Baru shrugged, standing up in his stirrups to look out over the low trees as though he were searching for a water supply. It was Amadu who replied. He seemed anxious to push on, and indeed had been furtively looking back and around most of the morning. Now he broke in.

"There is water ahead," he replied, "and we should reach it soon," and his long, expressive fingers marked a point in the sky where the sun should be by the time they reached it. Bill roughly reckoned on another hour at least, but feeling that water was necessary, he nodded, spoke to Baru, and the horses resumed their tired plodding.

When Bill felt that he would have to stop, he heard Baru shout. Digging his heels into his horse, he pushed up closer, where Baru and Amadu sat looking at a spot a short distance ahead. Riding up beside them, Bill saw what was taking their attention.

They were at the tip of a slight decline that seemed to be the bank of a dried up river. Across from their position, over the white sand that during the rainy season would be covered with water from the hills, was a large dark area, partly ringed with grass and small bushes. In the center of this could be seen three small antelopes, the duyker, their heads down, either eating or drinking. Amadu jutted out his chin.

"There is water," he said, "if the animals have left any." Then following Baru, he urged his horse over the bank and into the soft sand, the hooves soundlessly sinking up to the fetlocks. Baru signalled silence to the two men behind him, and gradually the distance between the horses and the animals lessened.

Suddenly a graceful head was raised, nostrils flared wide, ears moving ceaselessly back and forth. Slowly the head came around, the round brown eyes took in the approaching horsemen, and with one bound the animal cleared the water, and with another it had disappeared into the bush on the far side. The action was almost faster than the eye could follow, and at the signal the other two were not a whit behind. The men watched fascinated at the timidity, the power of these wild creatures. Baru grinned at the men. "Now we have the water to ourselves," he said, and swung stiffly down from his horse. The others followed suit, and soon the horses had been watered and hobbled in the luscious grass, and the men were splashing the warm water over their faces and heads.

Bill noticed how the two Africans washed their legs and feet first. It was always an amazement to him to see them do it, whereas he always washed his hands and face first. *Just another one of those differences,* he mused. *I guess they figure that it is the feet that must get them where they are going and therefore need the most care,* and he chuckled to himself.

Baru was building a small fire, and soon water was boiling. Bill offered to share his hot tea with the men. It was declined, both men being content with the contents of their gourd water bottles which they had filled with a thin, guinea corn gruel. On this they could subsist the day. Bill felt envious as he prepared his tea and took out the sandwiches that Jane had made for him. The rest of his food was in his chopbox, now some distance ahead of him, he hoped, the carriers of which he should catch by the late afternoon.

After satisfying their hunger and thirst, the men lolled for awhile in the shade of the trees. At least Baru and Bill did. Amadu was evidently impatient to get along, and soon his restlessness infected the others. The horses were unhobbled and they swung into the saddle once again. Another four hours' ride was before them before camp would be made for the night. They slumped in their saddles.

A shriek from Amadu startled Bill. His horse reared and plunged and only good horsemanship saved him from being unseated. He was busy for a few minutes getting control of his horse before he could take in the reason for the commotion.

A group of men had appeared like wraiths from the bushes at the side of the road, and Amadu was writhing and shouting in their grasp. He had been plucked bodily from the saddle, and his horse was already bolting past Baru and down the road.

Simultaneously the two riders were off their horses and racing to the aid of the hapless Amadu. But as they neared, more people came out of the bushes and stood between the struggling man and his friends. One of them barked out something to Baru, and he in turn called to the doctor.

"They say to stop," he called out. "They are of the tribe of Amadu." Then he walked closer and came to stand beside his white friend, while one of the men who seemed to be the leader came to them. He began speaking rapidly in a tongue that Bill did not understand, and Baru listened intently. Then he turned to Bill. "They are Fulanis," he motioned to the group of men and a now subdued Amadu, "and they have been following Amadu for nearly a month. They say that he has taken money that was from a cattle sale, and that all they want is to take Amadu back and to get their money."

Just then a man who had raced after the horse came back, leading it by the reins. The one who had spoken went over to it and untied the sleeping mat from the saddle. Unrolling it, he disgorged a small kettle, invariable accompaniment for the Moslem traveler so that he would be able to wash his hands, feet and face in ceremonial ablution, a few pieces of clothing, and a small package done up in some native woven cloth. This latter was picked up, unwrapped, and out cascaded coins and bills that must have added up to a great sum.

Bill stooped and picked up some of the West African pound notes that were fluttering in the breeze, then looked at the pile of coins. Finally he spoke to Baru:

"Tell him that we did not know Amadu was a thief or we would have turned him over to the chief in our village." He waited, while Baru interpreted. Then: "Ask him what he is going to do with the man."

Baru did so and then turned back to the doctor: "It is better not to ask, I suppose," he said, "but they will take him back and they will judge him among their own people."

"Tell them that is not wise," replied Bill. "Tell them to take him to the native court and justice will be done."

Again Baru gave the message, but the man only shrugged.

"I don't think they will," he said to the missionary, "and sometimes I can hardly blame them. This man," and he motioned to Amadu with disgust in his look, "went off with the money that was to be shared by all his people. They might have been left to starve for all he cared."

"What will they do to him?" asked Bill.

"At the least cut off one of his hands," replied the African. "That is the usual practice. Perhaps worse," and again he shrugged.

"Can we do nothing about it?" queried McAdams.

"Not unless we try to go back with them and get the chief to handle it," replied the other. "If they leave us here, they will carry out their own law in their own time."

Bill tried to think. To go on would be to leave this wretch to the mercy of his own people and their righteous indignation. To go back would be to leave his carriers, somewhere ahead, without any knowledge of where he was or what to do.

"Ask them," said Bill to Baru, "if they will camp with us tonight, and we will talk of this thing. Perhaps tomorrow we will return to the village and let the chief decide what should be done."

When Baru had transmitted this message, the Fulani leader was taciturn. Then turning he spoke to some of the other men, far too rapidly and with an idiom that even Baru's keen ears could not follow. Then the leader turned to Baru:

"Tell the white man that we will do as he says. Tell him his carriers are just ahead, resting in a hut that hunters have built in the bush. We can stay there tonight and return with you tomorrow. But we will tie and hold Amadu," and he shot a malevolent look in his direction.

The leader now climbed on to Amadu's horse, and leading the way, the other two horsemen fell into line. The men on foot, almost dragging Amadu, followed.

A scant hour later they came to the clearing and saw the cluster of rough huts, with Bill's bed bag and chop box outside one of them. The carriers were nowhere in sight.

Baru spurred ahead, dropping lightly from the horse as he neared the hut with the loads in front. Then looking in the doorway, he hastily drew back, and gesturing to the others to stop, he moved to one side of the opening, Then a great grin on his face, the fun-loving African put his hand across his mouth and soon there issued, first quietly, and then stronger and stronger, the coughing cry of the leopard. It was a realistic imitation and the missionary and Africans watched in puzzled admiration.

Baru was silent for a moment, then again he sent forth the bone-chilling sound, this time increasing its volume. He had just given a final cough when there was a sudden flurry from the hut and two boys hurled themselves out into the open, eyes blinking and faces almost blanched with fear. Beside the door, the leopard's cry went again. They whirled and saw Baru, his hand still to his mouth, shaking with laughter. Then the boys turned again and saw the other horsemen and began to grin foolishly. When one is asleep, the cry of the leopard comes to waken and stir the most sluggish blood into a pounding pulse. The people watching the play whooped in appreciation. Even Amadu managed a sickly grin.

Bill dismounted, and saluted his two helpers. Quickly he told them that they would camp there for the night and they nodded, the fear gone and only the occasional shamed glance shot at Baru indicated they had not forgotten his trick. Their turn would come.

Camp was quickly made, fires were lit, and Bill busied himself getting his own camp bed and roll ready for the night. The hut proved completely uninviting, and he went off to the bush to cut down four straight six-foot branches. These he lashed securely at each corner of his bed, and then with Baru helping him, he tied his mosquito net to it, making a white canopy over the cot. This would ensure a night free from mosquitoes, the one African plague that he could never get used to. The Africans were completely nonchalant and perhaps immune to them.

A simple meal, including the inevitable tea, soon satisfied his hunger, and he noticed that the Africans had also finished whatever food they had brought along with them. Now they squatted, hunkering down around the fire, to talk desultorily, breathing in the smoke and enjoying the heat as the sun quickly shot to the western horizon.

It was dark almost instantly. One by one the men rolled up in their blankets, and lying down with their feet toward the fire, were soon asleep. Only two men, left to guard a sleepless Amadu, remained up. Bill decided to follow suit.

Slipping off his riding boots, he undid the edge of his net and quickly slipped inside. It was warmer in there, but the privacy and freedom from the bug-filled night was a relief. Slipping out of his shirt and shorts, he piled them at the foot of the bed, crawled under the light blanket, and was soon asleep, the fatigue and heat of the day providing the best sleeping tonic that he could prescribe.

It was a shout from Baru that wakened him. There was still no sun, but the gray light of pre-dawn outlined the camp. Quickly pulling on his shorts, Bill raised his net and slipped out, reaching for his boots as he did so. Turning them upside down and knocking them together to dislodge any nighttime visitor, he pulled them on and was soon standing by the fire. The camp ground was empty. Every Fulani, and Amadu, had fled in the blackness of the night, slipping into the jungle like its own denizens, and gone to hold court in their own place and in their own way on their culprit.

Bill sighed. "Well," he said to Baru, "we tried. No sense in following them now. Poor Amadu."

Baru grunted, more inured to the ways of his country. "Steal and lose a hand," he commented. "After all," he went on, "the Bible says if a hand offends to cut it off. These Fulanis don't know about the Bible," he said, "but they do know it's wrong to steal. And since you steal with your hands . . ." and he made a significant cutting motion across his wrist.

"Guess you're right," replied McAdams, "but I would rather see justice done before the native court. Not a hand cut off," he added hastily as Baru grinned, "but punishment that is just for the crime." He shrugged. Then he turned his attention to getting his meager breakfast. There was much traveling to be done this day.

Twenty-three

With a spare horse to use, Bill dismissed his carriers and sent them back to the mission with a short note to Jane telling her about the events thus far on the way into this new country. It seemed strange to be sitting out in the bush, in the early light of morning, and writing back to someone at the station who cared.

Different from my last trip south, he thought to himself, as he wrote in such a way that Jane would not be worried about him. Then he fell to musing of that time when with Baru he had heard the bamboo sing, rescued Chuna from the Kitta people, and himself been badly mauled by the leopard. Then there was no one to whom he could write or call for help. Now he knew that both Jane and Pat would be anxiously waiting for some word from him. With a light heart, he wrote his account, throwing in the story of Amadu almost as a second thought and making no mention of the possible penalty awaiting him in his tribal court. *They will learn some of these gruesome things soon enough,* he defended his reticence to himself. "Sufficient unto the day. . . ." and he scrawled his "with all my love, Bill," at the bottom of the page.

When the men had set off on the return trip to the station, Baru and Bill busied themselves making a makeshift harness that would convert the extra animal into a pack horse. It was an ingenious system of grass rope devised by Baru. When it was finished, the two men took the hobbles off their own horses, saddled them, and quickly mounted. The sun was climbing overhead and the men wanted to be well on their way before its heat slowed their pace.

Baru, who was in the lead with the pack horse, was a son of the jungle, ever alert and listening as they rode along. Bill was content to slump back in the saddle, saving his energy for the mountain climb that he knew was so soon ahead. The sun rose higher and the heat became more and more intense as the horses plodded along, their hooves kicking up little puffs of dust that swirled up to the riders' throats and noses, forming an almost intolerable gritty surface to skin and clothes.

They almost stumbled on the village. It was the keen ear of Baru that heard the first faint ay-oooooooo that came along the valley, the all too familiar death wail that throbbed, rose, and fell on the still air. Bill jerked awake as Baru reined in and the three horses pressed close together.

The two men paused a moment, then as the cry filled the air the second time, they went forward on foot. A slight rise blocked their gaze from the valley ahead, and as they climbed it, Bill followed Baru's half stoop that made them blend in with the surrounding bush. At the crest, they looked down in surprise. Below them, about a hundred yards away and at the end of the long decline, lay a small village, its grass roofed houses packed closely together, making it little more than a large compound. Just outside the cluster of huts, they could barely make out a group of men and women, now jumping, now throwing themselves on the ground, and all the while, the ay-oooooo rang out, its faint echo coming up to the men.

Bill unstrapped his binoculars and focused them on the group, then silently passed them to Baru.

The men saw, propped against the last hut of the circle, what was evidently the corpse of the one who was being mourned in such a wild fashion. Two old women were leaning over the body, moving its legs and arms, flexing its back, keeping it supple against the *rigor mortis* that must have been setting in.

Immediately in front of the body knelt an old man. "It's the witch doctor, the *mai-tsafi*," said Baru quietly to Bill as he passed the glasses back again. "He is planting corn or rice in front of the dead, to make sure of food in the other life. In a little while they will dig a hole near where they are now and bury the dead one. We had better by-pass this town, for they will not be happy with strangers when there is a death celebration."

So saying, the two men slipped back to the horses, and back tracking a short distance, they cut off across the flat plain in a direction that would completely by-pass the small town.

Bill was alert now, and watched with amazement the sure and confident way that Baru led through the now pathless wilderness. His head was high, eyes ever alert, looking here and there, gazing straight ahead, and his flat nostrils flared wide as though he were smelling his way. Soon he made the turn that would bring them back on to the trail again, this time a good distance beyond where the people mourned their dead.

It was late afternoon by the time they were once again on the path, and Bill ached in every muscle. He spurred forward and rode alongside his companion.

"Do we stop soon, Baru?" he asked, as the other turned and looked at him.

"Soon, *Mai gida*," replied the other, "but we would be wise to make it to the base of the mountain and camp there for the night. Can you go that far?"

"I suppose so," he replied, grimacing as he rubbed his aching back. "When shall we arrive?"

Baru made an expressive gesture with his fingers. "When the sun is so," he said. Bill noted that it would be perhaps six o'clock with the sun in that position, looked at his own watch, and set himself for the next two hours in the saddle.

When he felt he could go on no longer and sharp pains were setting his legs on fire, he saw, with an audible sigh of relief, that they were breaking out of the sand and bush area and were passing great masses of tumbled rock. Baru looked at him with a grin and indicated that they would soon be where they could stop for the night.

"Not too soon for me," muttered the doctor to himself, then tried again to ease the stiffness of his saddle cramp. Even the excitement of what might lie behind the mountain could not compensate for the weariness and pain that he felt with every jolting move of his horse. When he felt he could go on no further, he looked at his companion, gritted his teeth and determined on another half hour as the limit of his endurance.

It was less than half that time when he saw Baru raise his hand, rein in his horse, and slide out of the saddle, no sign of weariness or fatigue showing in that compactly muscled body.

The doctor pulled his horse up, then stiffly lifted his leg from the stirrup, swung it gingerly over the pommel, and lowered himself slowly to the ground, the left leg in the other stirrup. The horse gave a slight start, jerking him away from the saddle, and twisting his foot slightly in the stirrup. In an instant, Baru was at his side, holding the horse, untwisting the foot from the stirrup, and letting the man stand, slightly bow legged and bent, while needles darted with incredible relief through his back and legs. Slowly he straightened, then grimaced at his companion.

"I have grown soft with life at my home," he said, as he

slowly flexed his legs and back, "but I see that you will soon harden me up for the road."

The other grinned back. "I forgot that you are not as my people," replied Baru, "who find that riding a horse is much better than the walking that we do mostly." He lifted his bare foot, cracked and calloused and hard as leather from its lifetime of walking the African paths. "I too must be careful, or else I will have to wear the shoes of the white men," and he gave a little prance that mocked his friend.

Bill laughed. "Where do we stop for the night?" and he gestured to the rocks strewn around them.

"We will look for a good spot," replied the other, and taking the reins of the two horses in his care, he stepped off the path, and led them up and over the rocks. Bill followed, walking slowly as the strength seeped back into his legs.

Baru's sixth sense had forecast accurately, and the men soon found an ideal camp site near a cluster of cottonwood trees. Some sparse grass that covered a flat area would be adequate for the animals for the night.

While Bill unsaddled the horses and hobbled them near the fringe of the grass, Baru went off to look for water. In about half an hour he was back with the news that he had found a small spring trickling out of the rocks. He gathered up Bill's collapsible canvas bucket and went off to fill it. Bill busied himself preparing the camp for the night.

When the men had satisfied their hunger, the doctor sat on the edge of his camp cot and Baru lolled on his sleeping mat.

"Tomorrow," he said, "we will travel with heaviness." He waved his hand to the south. "This path is the one that Amadu said would lead over the mountain. I do not know it, but it looks difficult. We should start early, when the sun is not up and the horses are fresh." He looked over to where one of them was rolling in ecstasy in the grass and sand. "Whether we can take them all the way I do not know."

"Let us get our sleep then," said Bill, "and since we do not know the way that we take, let us have prayer here that the great God will lead us, for surely He knows the way."

"Surely He does," replied the other. Then taking a battered Hausa Bible from his blanket roll, he looked up at his friend and asked: "Is there a passage that we can read before we pray?"

Bill thought for a moment, then remembered Pat telling of Peter Dunning's message. "Let us read the story of Jonathan and his armor bearer going over another mountain." He took

the Bible, leafed through the pages, and after some seeking found
the passage that he was looking for. Handing the Bible back,
he said to Baru: "You read it, and when you come to Jonathan's
name, put in yours and mine; and for the armor bearer, say
Ubangij Yesu Kristi, the Lord Jesus Christ."

He sat back and listened as Baru read the passage in his
slightly singsong voice. He closed his eyes and heard the man
mention their two names in the account of the mountain climbing. The story and its scene seemed to come alive. He opened his
eyes and as he did so, the slanting sun, now hastening to its
western rendezvous with night, shot its rays on the hill still
confronting them. A glory seemed to gild the massive rock that
now stood out in the strong relief of light and shadow. As
Baru finished, he bowed his head and prayed for the way that
they must take, the unknown road and the unknown people,
and claimed them for the Lord.

Twenty-four

The sky was a misty gray when Bill heard Baru stirring. With a groan he slowly and stiffly raised his net and rolled off the cot. Every bone and muscle ached, and he stretched tentatively, feeling the surge of blood and the relief of movement that swept over him.

Baru watched him, the old grin on his face. "Today you will get new strength," he said, rising from his hunkering position before the small fire that he had coaxed out of the ashes of the night before. "Your water will soon be boiled and ready for your tea." Then he went off to prepare his own cold and simple meal. "Perhaps tonight I will eat *tuwo*," he called over to the doctor, who was busy getting food out of his chop box. Bill could almost hear him smacking his lips over the anticipated guinea corn porridge and gravy that formed the invariable diet of his people. "Whatever I eat, I am never satisfied unless I have *tuwo* and *miya*," he had once told the doctor. His present diet of cold gruel and peanuts would only maintain strength, not satisfy his hunger.

It was still before dawn when the two men saddled their horses, hitched the packs on the back of the spare animal, and mounted. A short walk led them back to the path, and soon the horses were off on their easy canter, the motion easing the ache in the doctor's back and legs.

The path swung back and forth, wending its way between great boulders, and all the while ascending, until the horses were digging in their forefeet to gain their momentum for the next step. By the time the sun had broken over the line of hills far to the east, the horses were laboring, and finally Baru called a halt.

"It will be better if we walk them part of the way," he said. Suiting action to his words he dismounted and the doctor followed suit. Relieved of their loads, the horses snorted in freedom, then docilely followed the men up the gradual incline.

114

It seemed hours to Bill before Baru halted again. Their path now lay alongside the hill, and the missionary shuddered as he looked over the almost sheer drop at their side. One false step, and horses and men could be sent rolling and tumbling down the steep pitch of the mountainside. He inched closer to the comfort of the rising face of rock on the left. Baru was nonchalant as ever, his bare feet sure and safe on the narrow path. Even the horses were forced by the narrow path almost to criss-cross their legs as they paced. Yet there was never a stumble as with sure-footed eagerness they followed the men. McAdams took a deep 'breath, turned his eyes from the five hundred foot drop, set his gaze on the trail of the pack horse, and plodded on with the others.

It was impossible to stop on this narrow ledge, and the sun rose higher and higher as the path continued to wind and weave around the mountain.

It was mid-afternoon before they reached the summit, or what Bill thought was the summit. The narrow path had broadened, then flattened out into a great plateau, and with a sigh of relief Bill saw that at last they could call a halt. Baru had dropped the reins and was wandering around the flat area as though looking for something. Bill saw him go down on one knee, then drop to his stomach, his mouth cupped in his hands. From the distance, the doctor heard the muffled heave and, dropping his own reins, ran to where his friend lay stretched out. *Sunstroke,* he said to himself, as he ran, *sunstroke, or fever. Perhaps this altitude,* and he felt his own heart pounding in the lighter air.

By the time he reached his friend, the heaving had stopped, and he was sitting up, a puzzled look on his face. As the missionary dropped on one knee beside him, he looked up.

"I can't understand it," he said, cutting into his friend's question as to what was wrong, "I can't understand it," and a look of honest puzzlement spread across his features.

"Can't understand what?" asked the doctor, looking first at the African and then at the hole over which he had been leaning. "Are you sick?"

"Sick? Me? No," then he went off into a gale of laughter. "You thought I was sick!" he gasped in between gusts of laughter. "I was just trying to prove I was righteous," and again he howled, rolling over and over in glee.

"Righteous? Why. . . ." Bill looked at the hole again, and slowly his face relaxed into a grin. Then he was guffawing with

Baru. "Is it the hole Mohammed's camel is supposed to have made in the rock?" he asked when both of them were standing, laughter still in their eyes.

Baru nodded. "I knew that the holes his camel was supposed to have made were up here somewhere. When I saw this flat place and that hole," and he indicated the one where he had been lying, "I looked for the other, a camel's stride away. There it is," and he took three paces and tapped his toe into a similar hole. "But I guess I am not righteous enough to produce the water," he said. Then impishly: "Will you try, O righteous doctor from Canada?" and he waved his arm as though offering something to his friend.

Entering the spirit of the moment, McAdams dropped to his knees. Lying flat on his stomach, he formed a trumpet with his hands, fanning them out wide at the base to cover the mouth of the hole completely. He would test this Moslem myth with a good old school try.

He took a couple of short breaths to get as much oxygen as possible into his lungs, then turning his mouth out from his hand for a second, he gulped in a great lungful of air as he had been trained to do in the rough and tumble water polo he had played at University. Locking his hands again around his mouth and blocking the hole, he let the air go with all the pressure of his powerful lungs, creating air pressure that nearly deafened his own ears. Faintly there came a whoop from Baru, who was dancing in a frenzy beside the other hole.

"You did it! You did it!" He was shouting like a little boy. "See, here is water," and he patted his hands into a little pool that had gathered around the mouth of the hole.

Bill rose to his feet, slightly dizzy from the pressure he had exerted and perhaps the oxygen that he had inhaled. He moved over to Baru.

"Ai, you are the righteous one. You brought up the water as the legend says," and Baru patted his friend on the back. Bill looked down doubtfully, then was down on his knees again, his arm plunged up to the shoulder in the hole. As he pulled it up, it was dripping from the elbow to the finger tips.

"*You* dipped the water out," he snorted at Baru, flicking some water into his face from his fingers.

"*Gaskiya,*" the other looked hurt, "truly I did not. The legend says that a righteous man can produce water. You produced water. . . ."

". . . ergo, I am righteous," said Bill in English. The African looked at him blankly for a moment, then smiled.

"Try it once more," he replied, "and I will stay back with the horses. Then you will know what I already know — that you are indeed a good man," and he flung an affectionate arm around the shoulder of his friend.

"Not for me," said the doctor. "If you believe that I did it and am righteous, I will leave it there, lest you see that I fail. But one thing I know," and he patted the arm on his shoulder, "we have water, and I will have tea," and he turned back to his horse.

Baru looked at the hole with its edge damp from the fast drying water, looked at the missionary, then shrugged. It was beyond him. He followed to the horses and began to unsaddle and hobble them.

While Baru was busy, Bill tied a string around the handle of his cup, and with his canvas bucket beside him, began the laborious work of dipping out water from the hole, cupful by cupful. As he did, he tried to fathom the mystery of the water. The probable answer came to him suddenly, and taking the full cup up, he emptied it into the bucket, then got down on his knees again. This time he stretched his arm to its limit, until his fingers barely touched rock at the bottom. Moving his fingers around the base of the hole, he finally found what he was seeking. A small opening led in the direction of the other hole. Going to the first hole where he had blown the air down, he reached into it. About half way down he felt a small opening, and his finger in it was directed toward the second hole. He sat up with a satisfied smirk, the trick clear to him.

The dry hole had a small down-slanting channel that led to the water hole. When pressure built up in the first and pushed along this channel, it forced a small spout of water up to make room for the air. His complete conservation of air and an unconscious application of his knowledge of air pressure had produced his "righteous" water. He would explain it to Baru later. He went back to dipping his cupful of water.

Later, when the men were sitting back and enjoying the fresh breeze that swirled over the plateau, Bill tried to explain to his friend how water could come out of the one hole by blowing in the other. To no avail. The legend was deep in his mind, and finally the missionary gave up.

"All right," he conceded to his friend, "just as long as you don't think I am truly righteous because of this water business,

I don't mind going along with the myth. But I could get even you to produce water from the hole if you would do as I say." The matter was dropped.

The sun had dropped past the point where they would dare travel further, and the men decided to sleep on the cool of the plateau before trying the long and arduous climb down the other side. Baru went off to find some grass for the horses, while Bill busied himself setting up camp for the night.

When the sun finally plunged them into sudden darkness, the men were sitting around the small fire, each with his own thoughts. As their eyes grew accustomed to the darkness, Bill looked up. The stars were close enough to pluck, and the impression was so strong that his arm was half way past his head before he realized what he was doing. With a shamefaced grin he turned to see if Baru was watching. He wasn't. His eyes were wandering into the great void that lay almost at their feet. Bill followed his look. There, twinkling in the distance below them, were myriad lights, winking and dancing as the stars did over their heads. It was like looking into a vast global mirror that could recapture the heavens and lay it flat.

"Fire," was Baru's laconic comment when he saw the missionary looking down. "There is a village down there, and we could reach it before the sun stands in the middle of the sky," and his hands pointed straight overhead. "My friend," and he laid a hand on the arm of the other, "tomorrow is the unknown for us. We go to serve God. Let us ask Him for His help as we go," and suiting action to his words, the good fellow rested his kinkly poll on his arms that were folded over his knees, and began to pray.

The stars seemed closer, and heaven surrounded the missionary and his friend as, on the top of Bima, the Tangled Mountain, they prayed and committed themselves for the morrow. They were climbing up on their hands and upon their feet.

Twenty-five

The descent the next morning
was a heart-stopping cliff-hanger that was half slide, half ride.
Some places were so steep that Bill followed Baru in dismount-
ing, and holding the tail of the horse, skidded and slithered
down, the restraint keeping the horses from plunging ahead and
perhaps losing their own sure footing. They looked like giant
jack rabbits as, with forelegs stiff and hind legs buckled under,
they slipped and rolled down the incline.

The narrow path was well marked. On either side were the
giant thorn bushes that had doubtless given the Tangled Mountain its name. Once one of the horses slid against the thorn
bush, and the steel-like prongs ripped hide and hair for about
six inches along its haunch. The animal squealed, kicked out
at the bush, and only Baru's hold on its tail saved it from rolling
helplessly the rest of the way down the mountain.

It seemed an eternity before Bill saw the horses moving
more normally and noticed with relief that the ground was
leveling out before them. Soon the rocks and thorns had lessened,
giving way to the lush vegetation of the plain. Baru called a
halt.

"Let us rest, *Likita*," he said to his companion, "and the
horses are in need as well." He looked over the ground. Seeing
something that pleased him, he turned off the path and made his
way to a clump of trees that grew tall and luxuriant about a
hundred yards away. His instinct had led him truly. As Bill
caught up with him, he saw that the trees were growing at the
edge of a large pool. The African had already unsaddled his
horse and it was fetlock deep in the water at the edge, drinking deeply, while its master was bathing his feet and legs with
a comical look of relief on his face. It did not take the missionary
long to share the pool with the animals and his friend, and the
relief as the water hit his face and neck was almost sensual.

When they had cooled off, the men set about preparing their

respective lunches and talking about their approach to the town
that could not be too far ahead.

"We will enter when the heat of the day is past," said Baru,
his hand indicating a three o'clock sun. "Life is more normal
then for my African people, and they are easier to talk to. So
let us rest until it is time to go," and acting upon his advice,
he unrolled his ever present sleeping mat, closed his eyes and
was fast asleep in seconds. Bill looked at him enviously for
a moment, then finding a fairly smooth spot, he put his saddle
for a pillow and closed his eyes, waiting for the hour to pass.

He hadn't expected to sleep, but the quiet of the place, with
only the stamping and switching of the horses to break the stillness, lulled him off. He awoke to see Baru saddling his horse and
preparing the loads for the pack horse.

On seeing the missionary sit up, he grinned at him: "This
was to be a *siesta*," he said, using the word for rest during the
heat of the day, "not a real sleep." He dodged as Bill threw
a clump of earth at him, and sought refuge on the other side of
the horse. The two playfully threatened each other until the
horse began to sense the unusual movement and grew restless.
Baru moved out suddenly, releasing his hold on the horse's
bridle. At the unexpected freedom, the horse shied toward Bill
who moved away quickly, only to find himself balancing on
the low edge of the bank. He tried to recover his balance,
but felt himself slipping slowly into the water. Baru was rolling on the ground, gasping and choking in a paroxysm of laughter that rendered him completely helpless.

Standing calf deep in the water, Bill felt a first burst of
annoyance, then slowly a grin spread over his face. He squished
out of the water to join in the full-bodied laughter of his friend
who had tricked him.

When he had changed his socks and pulled on his damp
shoes again, the men busied themselves getting ready for this
important phase of their journey. It was two men, sobered and
quiet now, who swung into the saddle, made their way back to
the narrow path, and started for the village.

Again it was Baru who was in the lead, and after a canter
of a mile or so, he reined in until Bill had drawn alongside.
"Just ahead of us is a village cesspool," and he held an expressive finger beside his nose. "And the village will not be
far away from it."

Bill sniffed the air, but could detect none of the strange
odor that had warned his African friend. But as they kicked

their horses into a walk and proceeded along the path, the air became first tainted and then a powerful stench that gripped at the stomach of the horsemen.

Stronger and stronger it became. Then Bill saw the village latrine. It was a great pit, giving off its fetid odor and a peculiar blue light under the bright sun. As they neared it, a busy hummmm mingled with the odor and with his hand over his nose, Bill approached cautiously. As they reached the soggy edge of the pit, the blue suddenly rose up with an angry buzz, and the horses and men were almost immediately covered with a mass of great bluish-green flies which sought to settle wherever there was a clear stretch of skin or hide. The horses whinnied, as with tails high and switching they began to prance, then canter, while the men almost vainly sought to keep their eyes and mouths free from the pests.

"Whew!" said Bill as his hand made its ceaseless motion across his face, "what a hole! I bet there is more dysentery here than I've ever seen before. And plenty of other things too, I guess, with all these flies carrying disease into the town." The men put their horses to a quick trot. Soon the stench and the flies were left behind and they slowed their pace.

It was a good thing they did.

Rounding a bend in the road, they came upon a group of women in long single file, each with a great load of firewood on her head, looking back to see what galloped so quickly upon them. On seeing the strangers, there was a concerted shriek, the loads were thrown to the ground, and the women, naked legs flashing in the sun, shot off into the bush at the side of the path and were soon lost to view.

Not so their voices. Their cries and shrieks could be heard long after they had disappeared, and the men reined in their horses among the scattered loads of wood.

Baru looked grimly at the missionary. "I would rather not have frightened the women," he said at last. "I would prefer they were men. But when the women are roused, I would rather meet a wounded leopard on the road," and he looked so woebegone that Bill had to laugh at him.

"*Ba komi*," he said, slapping the other on the shoulder, "never mind. We will go forward slowly and they will see that we mean no harm or danger to them." And putting his heels to the horse, he moved off down the path.

Soon they were entering the outskirts of the village, its line of huts closely packed for safety and comfort against anything that the jungle might produce. Bill noticed that most of the huts were built of a combination of soft red stone and reddish mud. In front of most of them were red stone altars, and Bill caught a glimpse of some of them spattered with blood and what looked like dried porridge. Some had huge pots in the center of the altar, while others were bare, as though whatever was used for worship or sacrifice had been removed.

There was no sign or sound of people. Even the absence of dogs and chickens rendered an unnatural quiet in the village where noise and confusion are the order of the daylight hours and much of the night.

The horses wove between the huts, hooves falling in dull thuds on the rock that formed the foundation for the village. Bill turned in the saddle and looked back at Baru. The African was sitting easily and casually in his saddle as though all was normal. With the wave of a hand he motioned the other forward, and they continued on in unearthly silence.

About a quarter of an hour's ride took them completely through the village and, still obeying Baru's signal, they kept on riding until they were out in an open field, standing in the midst of corn that was just beginning to put forth green grass-like stalks.

Bill reined in, and the pack horse and Baru joined him.

"It is best to keep riding," said the latter. "If we had stopped, or shown signs of fear, or even given them the impression that we had come for any but peaceful reasons, we would have had an arrow or spear in our backs in no time at all. As it is, since they let us ride through in safety, we may be able to return, but not right now. They will want to have a palaver about it, and it would be best if we let them. We should go on for awhile and then we can make camp and return in the morning." Bill nodded, and once again they moved off, the horses walking slowly as though conscious of the unseen eyes upon them.

The path led into a small grove of trees, and soon the men were shielded from sun and spying eyes. Once more they held a council. "Let us go on until we find a good camping spot out in the open," said Baru, his lore coming to the fore. "Then if they come up near us in the night we will know." So saying, he dug his heels into the horse's ribs, lifted it into a canter, and led the way through the grove until they broke out on the other side.

He reined in so hard that his horse reared and settled

back upon its haunches. Bill's heart leaped as he too reined in. Then as the other horse settled down in a small cloud of dust, he saw Baru's hand motioning him forward. He moved to his side, and as he did so, he caught his breath.

They were looking at a pastoral scene, an African idyll. Framed in a great mass of bamboo clusters and mango trees was a little village, the huts sparkling white as though whitewashed, laid out in orderly rows. Between each hut lay a path, swept white sand giving it a glistening to match the white of the huts. The two men sat motionless on their horses, then waited tensely as they saw, coming out of a hut in the center of this scene, a man who walked slowly toward them. He walked with dignity, but not because of his clothes.

He was dressed in a pair of white shorts, clean and whole. On his back was an old bush coat such as Bill was wearing, but so rent and torn that it was impossible to see where the coat began or ended. The man continued to come toward the horsemen.

When he was a short way off, he called out something in a tongue that was completely unfamiliar to Bill. Baru too shook his head, then called out in Hausa:

"*Sannu aboki,* hail friend, we come in peace."

The man's face broke into a smile.

"*Aleikum salaam,* on you be peace," he said, saluting Baru and turning and giving a half bow to the white man. The latter put his horse to a walk and came near to the man.

"Do you speak Hausa?" he asked in that language. The man replied by saluting him for his journey, his tiredness, and his health. Then turning to Baru he repeated the same. Baru answered in kind, and then motioning to his companion he said:

"This is a *Likita,* a *Bature mai magani,* a white doctor who helps heal people's bodies. He also brings to us the message of God," and he pointed a finger heavenward.

At first the man was merely polite, but when he heard the last part of Baru's brief speech his face lit up.

"Does he speak the words of God and His Son Jesus Christ?" he asked, incredulity written all over his face.

As Bill heard the words "*Yesu Kristi,*" he leaned forward. "You have heard the news of Jesus Christ?" The question was full of unbelief.

For answer the man turned, and motioning for them to follow him, he turned back toward the village. The men followed.

As they neared the huts, the man called out something in his dialect, and men, women and children peered out of the huts. Some, with temerity, came onto the path. Bill and Baru looked at them in amazement.

The children were naked, but their sturdy bodies glistened and shone, showing no signs of the rickets or umbilical hernias that were so common among the people.

But it was the women who caught the eyes of the strangers. The ones that they had met on the road were naked, even with their heads shaved, and their bodies streaked with red ocher, with cruel tribal marks cut into the backs and chest. The welts had stood out even in the fleeting moment when the horsemen happened on them on the road.

These women, standing straight and proud, were dressed in sarongs, tucked tightly under the armpit, and handsome head cloths covered their heads. The few men who put in an appearance showed the same evidence of cleanliness, a sight that Bill never dreamed he would see in any village. Now here it was, buried on the unknown side of the mountain, a village that was clean.

The man who was leading them did not stop, but led them into the center of the town where there was the usual market square. The center of it was a giant baobab tree, and around it were piled in tiers some of the massive red stones that Bill had seen were used for hut construction in the other village. The man led them under the tree, then invited them to dismount. Bill did so, too stunned to feel the tiredness that would normally grip him as he got out of the saddle. When Baru had followed suit, the man motioned them to sit on the rocks, and as they did so, the people who had followed them gathered around, in a semicircle, looking with wonderment but no fear at the white skin of the stranger.

The leader of the group stood in front of them. Then he began to speak:

"You asked me a question on the road," he said, speaking to Bill, "asking me if I had heard the news of *Yesu Kristi*." He looked behind him and spoke in the unknown tongue. A little boy left the group and scurried to a nearby hut. The man turned back. "Three harvests ago," he said, his hands moving as he talked in the typical African manner, "I went over our mountain to trade my corn for some hoeheads and axes." Just then the little boy returned and thrust a cloth-covered package into the hands of the man. He fondled it for a moment, then took up his story.

"I came to a village of those who are called the Kitta people." Bill almost gasped aloud as he remembered his own experience there and how he had saved Chuna from those fierce people. The man went on: "There I became very ill, and my corn was stolen from me while I was sick with the fever. An old man, whose name was Tamanta, took me in," and Bill began to see again his own adventure in that tribe of fierce head hunters, and Tamanta, the old witch doctor, who had been so hard, then so wonderfully soft, and how he had rejoiced at hearing the news of Jesus, the Saviour. Bill's memory was going back and back. He was recalled to reality by the voice of the man standing before him. "Tamanta took me and cared for me as a father cares for a son." Bill nodded. He would. That is the way he had cared for Chuna who had married his daughter Salamatu. "And while I was sick," the voice went on, "he told me about a white man who had come and had saved the whole tribe from great trouble, and who also told about *Yesu Kristi*, who came to save all men from great trouble." The play on words amused Bill and he smiled. The eyes of the man were on him.

"Yes," replied the doctor to the unspoken question, "I was that man, and I came to this place to tell you the same news."

The man nodded, then taking the cloth parcel in his hand he carefully unfolded it and revealed a large book, bound in stiff cardboard. The missionary reached out a hand to take it.

"A Hausa Bible," he said to himself, and looked up at the man. He opened it at the first page. There was his own name, written years before when he had first come to the mission station to work with Peter Dunning. It was the Bible he had left with the illiterate Tamanta as a reminder that he had put his trust in the God who had given the Book. He looked up again.

The man went on: "Tamanta gave me the Book. He said it told about the way to God and about Jesus Christ. Then when he told more, I asked him what *juju* I must do to speak to this Jesus Christ. He told me there was no *juju*, no magic, no witchcraft. It was only to believe on Him and to let Him come into my heart." He used the African "stomach," and again Bill smiled. But he knew what the man meant. "While I was with him, I did so, and asked him many questions about this way of life, this Jesus path. And he told me all that you and Chuna had told him." The man paused. Then he took up his story as though afraid of saying too much.

"When I was better, I came home with this Book which he gave me. And every day I opened it, but the marks on the paper did not speak to me. One day my wife asked me what I did and then I told her. She said she too wanted to follow the Jesus path." He paused, then with downcast eyes, as though he was afraid of a rebuke, he said: "We could no longer do what our people did, and felt that we should move out of the village so that we could worship God without an altar or the help of the witch doctor. Since that day, these people have come here, and they too follow Jesus Christ." He looked around and there were nods and grins on all faces.

"How many do you have here?" asked Baru, putting in his first comment.

"There are thirty-nine of us in this *ungwa*, this small village," replied the other waving his hand to take in the clean and orderly huts. "And we try to live, waiting for the time when either Jesus or the white man would come to us."

Bill was dumbfounded. "Can you read this Book?" he asked, putting the Bible up for all to see.

The man shook his head. "No," he said, almost wistfully. "The black marks on the paper speak of God and His Son, but I do not hear them. Perhaps. . . ?" he looked plaintively at the white man and Baru.

Bill nodded. "Yes," he said, "I will read this Book to you. Then I will go back and send someone else to come, and you shall be taught to read it for yourself."

At these words a great huzza spread through the assembled people. After three years of looking at a Book, the black marks would speak to them.

Bill looked around at the spotless village. "What else have you done?" he asked the man.

"Come," he said, and led Bill and Baru through the crowd that parted to let them through. They were led to a small round hut that was set apart by itself on the edge of the market place. Pulling aside a grass mat, the man motioned the two strangers to enter. Straightening up after entering the low doorway, they stood stupefied.

They were in a hut about a dozen feet in diameter. It was freshly swept and its whitewashed walls glistened. On the floor were rows of small mud seats, about six inches high. At

the far end they saw a small raised mud platform. Bill turned
to look at the man who had now entered.

"What is this?" he asked.

The man shrugged. "In our other village we had a hut for
the demons of our tribe. When we came here we felt we should
have a hut for our God of heaven, a place where we could come
and talk about Him."

Bill's head was on his chest. These children of the jungle
had cut through to the simple truth: "Where two or three are
gathered together in My Name, there am I in the midst of them."

The man had gone to the front. On the platform was a
large clay pot. He reached into it and pulled out another
cloth that jingled. Bringing it back to the visitors, he opened it,
and Bill saw some old African coins, some cowrie shells, some
ornaments that had been used for the women's hair, and some
other unidentifiable items. Bill looked at the man.

"Every time we meet in here," he said naively, "we bring
something that we value, and offer it to our God. We have just
kept it here. Did we do right?" and the question almost trembled
on the good man's lips.

"You did right," was all Bill could say. Into his mind
swept the pictures of the people and churches at home, from
whom so little was demanded and so little given. Almost stum-
bling over the small doorstep, he went out into the sunshine.

The people were waiting with expectant faces. Bill turned
to their leader. "They call me *Likita* or *Mai magani*," he said,
"because I heal people's bodies. But I too worship this God
and His Son Jesus, and I am more anxious to help you know Him.
This is Baru," and he motioned to his companion, "who also
knows and loves Jesus Christ. And he can read from this Book,"
and he held up the Bible again, while the eyes of all were turned
almost reverently to his companion who looked embarrassed.

The man responded in kind. "I am Yepwi, the son of *Dan
baki*," he said, "and if you will stay and teach us, you will
indeed be a father to us."

Bill could only nod as he turned back to the tree. He
longed now for a quiet talk with Baru. All this was burning
like a fire in his brain. It was incredible, but what he was
seeing was true.°

° This account, in another part of Nigeria, was the actual experience of
the author and his brother in 1941. A flourishing mission station was erected
on the site a few years later.

Twenty-six

A sweaty face peered up
and back as Merle Wigle heard the voice at the door of the room
where he was working on the power plant. Standing in the doorway was Jane, a paper in her hand. Wiping his hands on greasy
trousers, he backed away from his awkward prone position,
straightened up, and came over to her.

"I have just received a note from Bill," she began by way
of explanation, "and I thought you would be interested in what
happened to him."

"Everything okay with him?" asked the older man anxiously.

"Everything is fine with him," she replied with a laugh,
"but he has been having adventures of sorts." Then unfolding
the sheet of paper in her hand she read the account of the capture of Amadu and the disappearance of the Fulanis with him.

"What will they do to him?" asked Wigle quizzically, "Cut
his hand off or something?"

"Oh, nothing like that, I hope!" replied Jane laughing
at his manner as he scratched his head thoughtfully. "But I
guess they can be cruel."

"Well" — the grizzled man dropped the question as he saw
Jane's peculiar look — "they most likely have a way of reducing
the thieving population somehow. Jungle justice. By the way,"
he went on, changing the subject, "I'll have most of this finished
in a day or so. Then I can wire the hospital and perhaps have
the whole thing working by the time Bill gets back," and the
man looked his satisfaction.

"Wonderful," replied Jane, looking blankly at the great
bulk of machinery. It was a complete mystery to her, and only
the end result would have any meaning. "I don't know when he
plans on getting back, but you should have another good week
at it."

"That will be fine," replied the man turning back to his
work. "In a week you will have more light and power than you
can use. This is one beautiful machine," and he caressed the
cold black metal lovingly.

Jane beat a hasty retreat. To love a piano was one thing, but this heavy, ugly machinery. . . . She cut through the hospital where Pat was busy with a couple of African helpers taking care of the morning run of patients. Jane looked in silence at the sight of this beautiful girl, leaning over a squirming black baby, whose leg from ankle to knee was a great, raw tropical ulcer. She saw the careful hands cleansing, powdering with sulpha, and then wrapping the leg, her easy movements calming the frightened child. By the time she had finished, the baby was lying quiet on her mother's knee. The nurse picked the little mite up in her arms and stood holding her closely for a moment.

"A tableau," whispered Jane to herself as she watched Pat, her white skin contrasting so strongly with the ebony black of the baby. She waited until the baby had been restored to its mother, then she turned and slipped away. How her heart ached for this girl who had surrendered so much in Michael Woods to come, nursing for Christ's sake. "Of such is the kingdom of heaven," whispered Jane, "of such is the kingdom of heaven."

The next week passed uneventfully. The power unit was working. Its lines had snaked into every part of the hospital, lifted on high poles to cross the compound, and was bringing the blessing of light to the two houses. Mr. Wigle had unpacked the iron lung, and it stood shining and rotund in its corner. He walked around checking his work and chuckling as he saw the African helpers switching lights on and off, awe on their faces.

"There it is," he said proudly to Jane, Pat, and his wife when the work was done. "And I don't think we have forgotten anything. If we have, we'll order it and get it immediately."

"Forgotten anything!" Pat just breathed the remark. "This is wonderful. When I first took over from Bill, I wondered how I would ever manage without power, then found I could do all right when I had to. Now this — " and she swept her arms around the small laboratory where they were standing. "And to have light at the flick of a switch . . ." and she suited action to her words — "Bill will be thrilled."

"No more than I am, young lady," smiled the man. "Now I have one more job to do," and he rubbed his hands in anticipation.

"Now, Merle," the habit of a lifetime could not be shaken, and the voice was loud and strident, "that there power is what you said you would do . . ." and then her voice dwindled away

as she saw her husband's face. "The chicks," she said at last.
"I had forgotten about the chickens."

"Right, Alma," and he looked as though he would slap
her on the back, then thought better of it, "my hatchery is next.
As soon as I can get that going, I'll get my men send us some
of the finest eggs in the world in our special packs, and we'll
get rid of the scrawny chickens I've seen running around here."

"You've been eating them too," his wife reminded him, "and
from what I have seen you've enjoyed them there chicks."

"Hah!" he snorted. "But the three of us have been eating
almost one apiece at a meal. Wait until you see a bird, basted
and brown on the platter, eating all you can hold and having
enough left over for another meal. . . ." and he smacked his lips
with exaggerated delight.

"And eggs you can trust," added his wife, who had had her
patience tested more than once trying to find some fresh enough
with which to cook.

The two of them pulled such faces that the girls chuckled
at them and their pantomime.

"Just make sure that one of the chickens is ready for Bill
when he gets home," admonished Jane. "One with at least three
legs," she added, then in a deep voice she went on: "Step right
up, ladies and gennulmen, see the only three-legged chicken in
existence. The only one in captivity," and suddenly found herself captured in the massive arms of Mrs. Wigle.

"Don't you talk about that there Merle of mine that way,
dearie," she said in mock severity. "If he says that he will
give you a chicken with three legs and four wings, that there
chicken will appear on your table," then her voice boomed out
in laughter as she released her captive.

The four of them made their way out of the hospital and
down the road toward the mission station. As they did so,
Pat drew back a little.

"Jane," the girl lowered her voice, "I've developed a terrific headache. Would you mind if I lie down for awhile? It
spreads all the way down my neck and back."

Jane was immediately solicitous. "Too much sun and re-
sponsibility all of a sudden perhaps," she said. "You go and lie
down and I'll bring you some tea."

They had slowed their walk, and Mrs. Wigle looked back.
Seeing the drawn look on Pat's face, she waited for them to catch
up. "Something wrong, dearie?" she asked, her keen eyes taking
in the slight wrinkle on the girl's brow.

"Just a headache," replied Pat.

"You take a couple of them there aspirines," and she gave her own peculiar pronunciation of her panacea for all aches and ills, "and lie down. If it is no better, I'll come and put cold cloths on your head. That always helps me," and the good woman was all tender solicitation.

Pat left them at the door of the house and slipped off to the cool dimness of her room. The pain was increasing, and she felt dizzy and nauseated. She knew it was more than just a headache, but did not want to bother her friends. Gradually she threw herself down on her bed, and with her arm across her eyes, tried to force back the pain that throbbed and ached. The pain and the heat both seemed to press down on her eyeballs, making them burn and smart. She tossed restlessly.

In a few minutes, Jane and Alma Wigle came into the room, one bearing a pan of water and a small towel, the other with a cup of tea. The sick girl sipped the refreshingly hot liquid, then lay back as the older woman, now tender and subdued, soaked her small towel, waved it for a moment to provoke evaporation and thus cool it, then pressed it gently over the forehead and eyes of the girl on the bed. There was a muffled sigh of relief from under the cloth, and the woman smiled. Jane left the room, to see an anxious Mr. Wigle standing in front of the tea table, his face full of concern.

"Is she all right?" the low voice was full of sympathy that made it seem more musical than ever.

"I think so," replied the other. "I wish Bill were here to look after her."

"Is there anything she needs?" he asked.

"Not unless you have an electric fan," the wishful thinking brought a smile to her lips.

"A fan? A f —" the man slapped his thigh. "Why didn't I think of that before. There is a crate of appliances that I ordered that can work off this generating unit," and grabbing his felt hat, he slammed out the door.

In half an hour he was back, a small boy bringing a bright toy to be shown around. In his hands he bore two oscillating fans, their bronze blades glinting in the afternoon sun. He patted them as he stood in front of an open-mouthed Jane.

"Careful now," he admonished her, "you'll swallow it if you open your mouth any wider." And he grinned his pleasure.

"Did you think of *every*thing?" she asked.

"I doubt it," he replied laconically. "But if I missed much

I'll kick myself." The two of them went into the sick room, where Mrs. Wigle was still putting the cloths on Pat's head and eyes. She looked up as they entered, and her own eyes opened wide.

"Merle," her voice was filled with surprise, "where did you get them there fans?"

"Got some more too," he almost boasted. "Where do we put these?"

At the conversation, Pat poked one eye out from under the cloth towel, then sat up in bed, the pain momentarily forgotten.

"Fans!" she whispered. "Fans, cool air," and she lay back again as the pain struck once more.

Mr. Wigle put one of the fans near the open window, plugged it into the shining new socket that he had put there such a short time before, and turned the button. The blades flashed quickly, then as though chopping up the hot air, they became a dizzy whirl, thrusting forth the air, weaving its head back and forth as though seeking out every corner and drawing the irresisting air into its clutch. For a moment the four people waited, then the air current struck the bed, went under, over and around it, its refreshing force breaking through the pall of heat that usually surrounded them. All four sighed simultatiously. And in its cooling freshness, Pat slept.

Twenty-seven

Pat had never known what it was like to be really sick, and the feeling of helplessness that grew day by day was almost more than she could stand.

She told Jane where to find some codeine and how to administer it, but still the pain and headache continued, increasing in intensity, if that were possible. Her whole body ached, it seemed, like a mechanical toy that must be wound up or moved before it went into action, and the pain began to go in spasms and jolts that she found difficult to describe. She found it harder and harder to move. At the end of the third day, she turned to Jane.

"Jane dear," the other was immediately alert and slipped to her side, "I don't know what I have, but I'm afraid it is something serious. When will Bill be back?"

"I don't know," replied Jane. "He has been gone two weeks now, and I'm sure that we can expect him soon. Would you like to have Mr. Wigle take you into Jos?" she asked as the solution flashed into her mind.

"I doubt if I could stand the jolting," the other's voice was almost a whisper. "It hurts to try and turn in bed," and she grimaced as another spasm jolted her.

Jane tried to make her comfortable, then slipped out of the room. Mrs. Wigle was pacing idly to and fro, waiting her turn to go and sit with the patient. She turned as Jane came out of the room.

"Alma" — several days before she had insisted that she be called by her first name — "I think that I will have to send word to Bill. He may be on his way home — oh, I *hope* so," and her eyes filled with tears, the strain of the past two days beginning to tell on her. Her own time in this country had been so short, and she was not yet inured to the rigors of the tropics and what they can do. The motherly arms were around her instantly.

"I suppose that Merle couldn't drive down to meet him?"

Jane smiled. "It is just a path and Bill was fortunate that a horse could travel it," she explained. "No, the only way would be to send someone down and either meet him or find him wherever he is." Suddenly she had it, and in a moment she was out of the house.

"Garba! Garba!" she called, "*Zo nan mana,* come here, come here."

A sleepy Garba poked his head out of one of the square, mud brick houses at the far end of the compound. Seeing the doctor's wife standing there, he quickly pulled his *mayafi* blanket around him and, still yawning, walked across to where she stood.

They saluted each other, the African between yawns. Then in her halting Hausa, Jane explained about the nurse, *Mai jinya,* being sick and their needing the doctor. Did he know the way that had been taken?

Garba did.

Would he be able to take a note to the *Likita* wherever he might be?

Garba could. His answers were brief and to the point. He turned back into the house, and in a moment was out, rolling up a sleeping mat with his blanket inside it, ready for the road.

Jane looked at him in amazement. Not that he was ready so quickly, but that he was so willing. She had yet to learn of the close tie between these Africans and her husband, and couldn't see into the heart of this man who would have gone anywhere for his brother Baru or the white doctor.

She slipped back into the house and hurriedly penned a note to Bill, describing the symptoms as best she could and asking for his advice or presence — the sooner the better. She closed with: "We — I miss you, Bill, and want you back. But I know your work. Do as you think best." She was just writing her, "Love, Jane," when she remembered and scrawled a hasty P.S.: "And when you do come we have a real surprise for you," then signed a single J.

Returning to the compound yard, she found Garba with his sleeping mat on his head, the usual long-necked gourd of drinking water slung over his shoulder, and a spear in his hand. He was ready for the road.

Jane handed him the note, and he slipped it into a pocket hidden somewhere in his torn shirt. Then saluting her briefly, he swung down the path, through the cactus hedge and toward the town. She watched the preposterous sight of the sleeping mat marching along the top of the hedge, then turned back into the house. Her heart seemed lighter now that she had sent for Bill. He would be home soon and look after Pat.

Entering the living room, she noticed both of the Wigles sitting near the doorway to the bedroom, hands clasped and their heads bowed. Jane was just in time to hear him saying: "And God, we have just begun to learn about You and Your work. And here is someone sick who is willing to live her whole life for You. Make her better, show us what to do. We ask it for Jesus' sake."

They looked up, somewhat sheepishly, to see Jane watching them, tears in her eyes. "Guess we haven't done enough praying," said Merle by way of explanation, "and it's too bad we have to start when there is a real need. But Alma and I were just saying that from now on we would be praying and working as long as you folk will have us here."

"I don't know what I would have done without you," said Jane quietly. "If it will encourage you, I think that the Lord has planned all this His way, and His ways are past finding out." The couple beamed at each other, then started as they heard a groan from the other room. The two women hurried in. Pat was leaning over the side of the bed, retching and vomiting. Mrs. Wigle reached her first, unceremoniously spilt the water from her basin on to the cement floor, and holding the girl's head, waited for the next upheaval. Jane picked up the cloth that had been on Pat's forehead and carefully wiped the sweating face, pushing the lovely hair back on her forehead. Pat gave a gasped: "Thanks," then sank against Mrs. Wigle's bosom, completely spent.

Jane slipped out of the room, to see Biriskilla standing and looking at Mr. Wigle, while he returned the friendly stare. "Biscuits" — the playful nickname slipped out — "bring me some warm water and cloths, please. *Mai jinya* is sick and I want to clean up a mess." The girl slipped away on her errand and Jane turned back into the room.

Oh God, she prayed silently as she entered the room and felt the stirring of the air from the fan, *oh God, bring Bill quickly*. Then she joined her friend at the bedside. Pat seemed to be asleep.

Twenty-eight

Bill and Baru spent two days at Angwa Takwa, as they learned the name of the village to be, sitting for hours with Yepwi and the little band of believers, talking to them, encouraging them, praying with them.

Both of the men were wise in their restraint. The wholesome, clean, and godly people needed not a lot of orders and restrictions for their lives and work. Somehow God had broken through to them and in the ordering of their lives, and with the worship that they gave, the men could find nothing wrong. The childlike simplicity, the faith that knew but could not see — all these spoke volumes to the two visitors.

"This is true worship," said Baru, during the first night when the men were resting in the clean and airy entrance hut to Yepwi's compound. "Without reading and without leaders, they have followed Jesus and serve Him. It is good?" and he asked the question in the darkness.

"It is good, Baru," replied the other. "When God speaks to the heart it is enough. This is the way He worked in the days we read about in the New Testament. I never expected to see it today."

"What do we do now, O my friend?" went on Baru.

"I think that we should go ahead with our plans before we came down here," answered the other. "Let us help and encourage them here for another day, then we will go back and plan on sending someone to teach them to read. Perhaps Pat will come here, and then one of us can be in or out all the time until *Mai Gida* Peter Dunning gets back."

"That is good," said the other. "It gives me a 'white stomach.' With *Mai molo* at the mission you will not need me so much, and I could come and live here during the dry time."

"We will see," replied the other. "Let us get some sleep, and tomorrow we will ask Yepwi if we can visit the village that he left to come here. I would like to meet the chief and some of the people. They need help too. Perhaps I can give some *magani*, some medicine, and they will see that we only want to help them." So saying he rolled over in his cot and was soon fast asleep.

The next day the two visitors, together with Yepwi, made their way on foot back to the village, where this time there were signs of life and activity. Coming in on foot and with the familiar Yepwi with them, the visitors seemed to arouse less fear in the people, although the children and the women slipped into the huts, to peer out with only the whites of their eyes showing.

Yepwi led them to a massive mud-walled building in the center of the town. Here half a dozen men lolled at the entrance and as soon as they saw the white man and his friend, they rose and stood as though guarding the way.

The two strangers hung back a little and let Yepwi go on ahead. He saluted the men and then spoke to them in the singsong language that Bill had first heard the day before. The men answered him in kind, and then one of them slipped inside, while the rest remained clustered at the doorway. In a moment he returned and said something to Yepwi, who turned and motioned his friends to come closer.

They were the cynosure of all eyes as they walked slowly forward. The men parted and let them walk on through and into the entrance hut. There they were met by two more men, these dressed only in loin clothes, while on their arms were wicked-looking knives, held in place by decorated leather bands. As the men approached, they turned, and the three followed them out through the other door that led to a courtyard. At the far end they saw a small booth, and under its shadow, sitting regally on a huge leopard skin, was the one whom Bill knew to be the chief. They went forward, and as they did so Baru and Yepwi bowed before him, while the latter spoke in the tribal tongue. He was doubtless explaining the reason for the presence of the strangers in their midst, for the eyes of the man swept between Baru and Bill. They were kindly eyes, wrinkled at the corners, gleaming with intelligence and wisdom. Bill took to him at once, and as soon as he saw it was a propitious moment he stepped forward and greeted the man in Hausa. It was a relief to hear him answer in the same lingua franca of West Africa. Soon the two were talking together, the chief keenly questioning the white man and Bill replying with candor. After a few moments, the chief called out something, and one of the servants brought some stools and set them in a semi-circle before the ruler. He motioned to the visitors to sit down, and they did so, with Yepwi showing the surprise that he felt.

Bill was speaking about his work on the other side of the mountain and how he sought to make people well, to help children, and above all to teach the people the way to the God of heaven.

All the while the wise old man nodded his head as though in complete agreement. Finally he spoke: "Your words are good; and I feel that you are a man who comes to help our people. The words of God I have heard before," and he nodded in the direction of Yepwi, who sat amazed. "No, Yepwi did not speak to me, but I knew what went on in my village, and what Yepwi has done is good. His *ungwa* is clean, his people are well, and their way of life is good." He turned to Bill. "You say you would like to come here and help my people? If you do, I will welcome you, just so you come in peace. I will send word that you are to be helped, and when you do come, you have only to ask and we will give you what you need. Yepwi" — and at the sound of his name, the man fell on his knees in a squat, the posture of respect for the chief — "Yepwi, you will be responsible for the *Likita* here as long as he is on our side of the mountain. I will send word out that you will stand in my place beside him." Then he rose to his feet, the interview at an end. Bill rose too, and the two men stood taking each other's measure for a moment. Bill saw a tall, handsome African, his green turban adding stature and dignity to the fine aquiline features. His eyes were calm and meditative, the eyes of a sage.

Impulsively Bill thrust forth his hand, thumb up. The other placed his with thumb up against the white man's and they grasped each other's thumb. It was the handclasp of brotherhood, and they held it for a moment.

Then Bill dropped it, saluted the man once again, and turned to leave. Baru and Yepwi followed suit, without the handclasp of equality, and the three were soon outside.

As they moved away from the entrance hut, followed by one of the servants to whom the chief had spoken in a rapid fire command, they heard him speaking to the men at the entrance hut, and they in turn immediately spread out into the village. Yepwi let his breath out with a swoosh. He turned to Bill.

"*Likita*," he said, grinning from ear to ear, "this is a great victory. He has sent messengers out into the village to tell them about you and to command your safety, and to give me the power to help you." His grin grew wider. "This is the first time that I have been to see him since we left the village, and I was afraid. Now the words of God can come here, and all the people will hear. This is a good day," and the fellow gave a little skip and jump in sheer delight.

Bill and Baru felt no less elated. Surely they had gone beyond the tangled mountain, and now their work could go ahead.

That afternoon and evening they spent speaking to the little group of believers. On the morrow they would be up at dawn and start back to the mission station. With Yepwi interpreting, both Bill and Baru spoke of the things of God, told them what was in the Bible that they had almost worshiped in their ignorance, and then sang some simple hymns that the people soon picked up. A sliver of moon was riding high when they finally broke up, and Baru and Bill were able to get away for a few hours rest.

How different was their trip through the town in the early dawn the next morning. While the people were silent, they were not antagonistic, looking up from their small smokey fires as the horsemen, with Yepwi walking in the lead, passed through the village.

They were not led past the cesspool this time, much to Bill's relief, and almost before they knew it they were at the base of the mountain.

Here Yepwi was to leave them.

He put his hand on the pommel of Bill's saddle. "Last night as I spoke to the God we worship, I thanked Him for sending you and Baru to us. Now we have a new day. We will learn to read the Book that talks, and all my people will hear of *Yesu Kristi*. Friend, go with God, and may He carry you back to us soon again."

Bill looked down at the honest face. "Either Baru or I will come back soon," he promised, "and later my friend the *Mai Gida* from the mission will come too. We will bring medicine and someone to teach you to read, and the Word of God will capture your village." Then calling Baru closer, he asked him to pray for Yepwi and the thirty-nine Christians, for the journey that they were about to take, and for the work to be done in this place.

So sitting on his horse, with Yepwi's hand still on his pommel and Baru's horse almost touching them both, the three men prayed while Baru's voice carried over the still country-side. It was a benediction indeed.

Yepwi was still standing with hand upraised when the first turn in the upward trail took them out of sight. Bill sighed and settled into the saddle for a long ride home.

It seemed no time at all before they were at the flat plateau again, and Baru pointed mischievously at the holes where Bill had proved his righteousness. Bill responded briefly. He was in no mood for a joke, and seeing his face set into thought-ful lines again, Baru was silent.

How different was the journey back down the hill, and the horses seemed eager now that they were on the homeward stretch, although it was a long way off. They picked their way sure-footed and delicately on the dangerous path plastered along the side of the mountain, and Bill was too preoccupied to give more than a passing glance at the drop away at his feet that had brought a twinge of fear on the trip up.

By the time the sun had fallen over toward the late after-noon, the men were nearing the bottom of the mountain, and Baru was looking out a place to camp for the night. He found it soon after leaving the rocks and bushes of the mountain, and Bill was enjoying the hot tea that he had come to enjoy so much. The horses were unsaddled and the pack horse's load was off when suddenly the three of them lifted their heads and whinnied. Baru was on his feet immediately, his instinct telling him that something strange had disturbed the animals.

He walked toward them where they were cropping grass near the edge of the path, and looked around. Then he heard what the animals had smelled. Someone was coming along the path from the north. He waited, his fingers entwined in the mane of his horse. Then he jumped so precipitously that his horse shied away, reared back, and being hobbled front leg to back lost its balance and rolled on to the ground. The commotion brought Bill to his feet in time to see Baru racing down the path. In a moment Bill was by the horses and saw Baru throw his arms joyously around a man who had just turned into the trail. Even from the distance he could tell the squat, muscular figure. It was Garba.

Slowly he sauntered down to meet the traveler, who by this time was coming his way, walking with his brother. When they came within speaking distance, the newcomer gave his short squatting bow, then began saluting his friend. Bill replied in kind, and by the time they finished, they had reached the camp site. Then Garba remembered his commission.

Digging into the riga shirt that seemed never off his back, he pulled out a crumpled and somewhat smudged letter, handing it first to his brother, as was the custom, and then saw it passed over to the doctor, whose heart leaped as he recognized the handwriting. It was from Jane.

With almost nervous haste, he slit the envelope, let his eye scan the brief message, then read it again, more slowly.

He looked up. Baru was watching him. "It is from *Mai molo*," he began to explain. "She says that the new one, the *Mai jinya*, the nurse, is very ill, and they do not know what more to do. They ask me to hurry back," and he thrust the letter into his bush jacket pocket. He turned to Garba.

"How did the *Mai jinya* seem when you left?" he asked.

The man merely shrugged. "When *Mai molo* told me she was sick and that they wanted you to come *maza maza*, I said I would bring you back. I know no more."

Bill paused, then turning to Baru, he said: "Once more we need to travel fast. Can you see the way by the darkness if we leave now?"

Baru looked up at the darkening sky, then at his friend. "We have traveled at night before when we had to," he replied, "and we can do it again for the *Mai jinya* who is sick. Besides," he added, pointing to the southeast, "we will have some of the moon to journey with us," and he pointed to the sliver of silver in the sky. Bill needed no further word. He turned to his chop box which was lying open, put in the things that he had taken out, and then with Baru got the pack on to the back of the third horse. Then he remembered Garba.

"Will Garba go with us?" he asked of Baru as they wrestled with the ropes.

Baru looked up. "Garba can ride on top of this pack until the horse gets tired, then he can rest. He will follow behind us, but without the loads we can travel much faster." Rapidly he spoke to Garba, who merely nodded. Whatever his brother said was all right with him. And a horse to ride was better than walking. Yes, he was agreeable. Besides he was at home in the bush as in the village. "*Ba komi*," he said to the missionary, "it doesn't matter. I will come along as the horse is able."

They were soon ready for the road, and with a farewell salute to Garba, the two men lifted their horses into a mile-eating canter and started down the darkening path. Soon the slight moon and stars would outline the sand of the path. Bill was grateful for the rest they had enjoyed. With the horses fresh, they would be at the mission before dawn, barring any unforeseen circumstance. With the wind ruffling through his hair, he rode as fast as he dared, to spare the horse on the dangerous road. He heard Baru's horse close to the rear. Darkness came, and with it the faint light of moon and stars. The horses sped on without slackening speed. Both of them felt the sense of urgency.

Twenty-nine

Jane had fallen into a light doze in the folding chair in the early hours before dawn when she heard the commotion on the compound. Rising groggily to her feet, she moved to the living room and then to the door leading outside. As she did so, it was pushed in, and framed in the doorway was a dusty, worried-looking Bill. At the sight of him her tiredness vanished, and with a little smothered cry, she threw herself into his arms.

"Oh Bill, Bill, you're here," the words were muffled against his shoulder. "Thank God you are here."

A tender hand turned her face up from his shoulder and in the dim light she saw the eyes of her man, looking down at her with his heart laid bare.

"Jane," he stooped slightly to kiss her, "Jane dear," and again he brushed her lips.

She pulled herself away. "Come in and wash up, then do take a look at Pat. I'm worried sick."

She turned and pulled him into the bedroom and over to the washstand. She poured the water from the big enamel jug, and stood back as he washed. Ever the doctor, she noticed the careful brushing of his fingers and hands, the peculiar bent elbow motion with his hands upraised as he looked for the towel. He was scrubbing his face when he heard a gasp from Jane. He pulled the towel quickly from his face, then dropped it to the floor in amazement. Standing framed in the doorway was a man of medium height, his crop of iron gray hair more tousled than ever. It was Mr. Wigle.

Bill stood with such a queer expression on his face that both Jane and Merle began to laugh quietly. In a moment the two men were grasping hands, and a flood of questions flowed from Bill.

Jane raised her hand. "You will hear it all in good time," she said, "in the meantime, there is Pat," and she put her hand

143

on his arm to lead him. "Come on, Mr. Man, there is work for you to do," and followed by the rumpled Wigle, they went to the other bedroom.

As they entered, Bill felt the stirring of cool air, and wondered at it on such a still, hot night. Suddenly he was blinking in a room filled with light, and he looked for its source. Hanging from the center of the room was an electric fixture. Jane merely murmured, "The Wigles," then switched off the light. She had seen Pat's impulsive move to protect her eyes from the light. Bill moved to the bed, his mind a jumble of thoughts.

A small lamp was barely glowing beside the bed, and Bill asked Jane for more light. As she went to bring a small pressure lamp, Bill sat beside the bed. Quietly he spoke:

"Pat, it's Bill, and I want to see what is making you sick." He felt the start of the girl under the covers, then a hand came out, feeling for him, and he imprisoned it in his big fist. The hand was hot and dry, and he needed no thermometer to tell him of the fever raging in the body. He continued to talk quietly, not giving the girl a chance to speak, until Jane brought the light. When its light fell on the face of the girl, he almost gasped. Only the steely self-control that had come through years of practice kept him from letting the emotion show.

He had left a bright, sparkling-eyed, beautiful girl, the day he had set out to go south over the mountain. Before him now was a sunken-cheeked, hollow-eyed girl, her head held back in a peculiar fashion. After the moment of surprise, he was the doctor again.

His questions to the patient were answered, sometimes in short jerky sentences, sometimes by Jane who stood quietly behind him. Bill's heart grew heavier and heavier.

It looked suspiciously like sand flea fever. Then he turned to Jane:

"Has she been up at all? Can she walk?"

"Not for the last twenty-four hours," replied Jane. "Yesterday she got up and just sprawled on the floor, and Mrs. Wigle and I had to pick her up and get her back to bed again. She says the headache is getting worse, and that she aches all over."

Bill chewed his lip, then almost on inspiration the symptoms fell into place and a great suspicion crossed his mind. Leaning back, he pulled the sheet from the foot of the bed, exposing the two white twitching feet of the patient. He scratched the sole of the foot with his finger nail, watching Pat as he did so. There was no reaction, no reflex. He threw the cover down again and rose to his feet.

"We will have to get her over to the hospital. I want to do a spinal tap right away. Can you and Mrs. Wigle get her into a housecoat so she won't get chilled outside? Wigle and I will bring a camp cot in and we can use it for a stretcher." He turned, purpose in his step and heaviness in his heart. Was he too late?

In a few minutes he had the cot ready, and he and Mr. Wigle were back in the room. The doctor merely nodded to Mrs. Wigle who was sitting on the bed, holding the girl's head close in a motherly embrace. With her help they lifted Pat, who seemed inordinately stiff, on to the cot, then he and the other man picked it up, and with Jane going ahead with a light, they moved out of the room, through the door, and out into the open air.

A group of Africans immediately sprang forward, Baru and Garba, who had scarcely dismounted from his horse, first. The men surrendered their burden, and with a word to Baru to be careful, he sprinted ahead to the hospital. He wanted to get the pressure lamps lit and the sterilizer on. He had so little time to lose.

His long legs had carried him nearly to the hospital when he heard the patter of feet behind him. Following hard were Jane and Merle Wigle.

"Bill, Bill," Jane was calling between gasps, "wait a minute. There are some things. . . ." He didn't listen nor stop to hear. With a bound he was up the familiar steps, turned into the laboratory immediately on the right, his hands outstreched for the familiar light and matches that he always kept handy. They were missing. Impatiently his arms moved in a circle. As they did, he heard the steps of the others outside, then a panting Jane was in the room.

"If you would only listen," she was saying, and then the room was bathed in light.

Bill looked around in amazement. Wiring was still in evidence, and everywhere he saw the plugs and switches that Mr. Wigle had put in so recently. Bill felt his own head swimming.

"Okay, little lady," he said, smiling down at his wife, "lead the stranger around his own hospital. Get the lights on and get Pat into one of the side rooms. I'll be there in a moment." He was collecting the equipment he would need. He gathered the fleeting seconds into his skilled hands and made them work for him.

The spinal tap was finished when he heard Pat gasp: "I can't breathe! My legs, my chest!" The cry was pitiful; the sweat was pouring down her face. Bill's head fell on his chest. He didn't need to test the spinal fluid. His suspicion was correct. He looked at Jane helplessly for a moment.

"Polio," his lips formed the word for her to see, then he was over the patient, slowly and rhythmically putting pressure on her chest, then releasing it. In, out; in, out; he began to sweat with the exertion and the agony of frustration.

For a moment she breathed easier, and Bill looked up. Mr. Wigle was standing near him. Then a great light dawned on the doctor.

"The lung?" he whispered the question. "Did the lung come?" The man merely nodded and motioned toward a room across the hall. In a bound, Bill was there, looking in amazement at the great oblong box, its chrome and mirrors winking in the light. He was back beside Pat.

"Quick, Wigle," he barked his orders now. "Get the power on that machine." He put his powerful arms around the girl, now moaning again with the strain of breathing against the creeping paralysis. Holding her straight and easily, he carried her to the room where the lung was beginning its thump, thump, thump, which they were to hear for weeks to come.

Jane followed with the cot, and for a moment he set the patient down, while Jane stripped off the dressing gown, leaving her clad only in the light nightdress. While she did so, Bill pulled the cot-like bed from the machine, rolling it out easily on the runners. By that time Pat was struggling for breath again, her hands feebly fluttering to reach her throat. Bill imprisoned them in his own, then picking her up again he turned toward the mechanical lung that could mean life or death for her. He laid her on the cot, then with the help of Mr. Wigle, they tenderly worked her down into it. The men were a trifle awkward, but the gasping of the girl gave impetus to the work.

A sponge rubber collar had to be fitted around her neck, with only her head protruding from the great metal box. When she seemed secured, her head resting on a soft mat and the great collar touching her chin, Bill moved to the gauges at the side. Sure hands touched one here and one there, and all the while the steady rhythm of the artificial lung was music to his ears.

Back at the head again, he looked down at Pat. The terrible strain and gasping were gone. For the first time that night she was breathing regularly and quietly. Bill's hand went across his sweating brow, a hand that now shook from strain and fatigue. A few hours before he had been riding wildly into the night. Now he stood and looked down, and thanked God he had not stopped.

He turned to Jane. "One of us will have to be here night and day," he said quietly. "Four six-hour shifts — that is, if you are up to it?" he questioned the older couple.

"We'll do it," replied Mrs. Wigle, as usual speaking for both, although her husband nodded. "And I'll take the first watch tonight. You look beat," she said to Bill, "so just tell me what to do, and then off to bed with you."

Bill explained how the lung operated as simply as he could, showed the others how to work it manually if the power should go off, then left word that he must be called immediately if anything unusual happened. Then he turned and left the hospital, the ground scarcely felt beneath his tired, dragging feet.

Thirty

Pat could only remember the fitting of the collar, and for the next several weeks when her life hung in the balance, there was no recognition, no sense of time.

And all this while, the four friends, sometimes joined by the faithful Baru, would sit for hours at a time, watching, almost counting every breath.

Never were the four together at one time, but bit by bit, the story of the Wigles and the tale of Bill's trip to the south were told.

During the second week of crisis, Bill had sent Garba back to the railhead with the news of the girl's condition, and a cable to be dispatched to Peter Dunning. He held out little hope for her recovery and none at all for complete recovery. The paralysis had been too violent and too complete, and his experience with it told him to fight but not to hope. In his cable, he told Peter to tell Michael Woods what had happened. He could imagine the anguish to those two dear and close friends.

The six weeks became seven before Pat showed any consciousness of those around her. Then one day, Bill was called by a fluttery Mrs. Wigle.

"Bill, come quickly," and he raced into the room fearing the worst. Standing at the head of the machine was Mrs. Wigle, looking down into the mirror that reflected the girl's face. And in that mirror were two eyes looking straight and true, and almost the hint of a smile on the lips.

He leaned over the girl. "Pat, if you can understand me, blink your eye," and he looked into the mirror. Deliberately and slowly the right eyelid moved over the eye, closing it for a second, then flashed open again.

"Can you speak to me?" he asked, mouthing his words slowly as to a little child.

The mouth worked spasmodically for a moment, then, to the rhythm of the giant respirator, she said, "Where . . . is . . . Jane?" The talk exhausted her and her eyes closed in weariness.

148

Mrs. Wigle left immediately to call Jane, who was sleeping after her recent watch, and soon the two came running into the room.

Bill told her that one crisis was passed and told her what had taken place. Jane leaned over the girl's head, looking into the mirror.

"Pat, Pat," she whispered softly. The eyes in the mirror opened slightly, the lips smiled, and then closed as the girl slept.

The three stood looking down at her for a moment, then Bill left instructions with Mrs. Wigle and he and his wife left the room.

In the hall she turned to him. "What is it, Bill? Will she ever get out of that thing?"

Bill shrugged. "I have no answer to that. She is coming into another crisis now, and we're going to have to pray and work harder than ever," and he put his hand under her elbow, and turned her to look at him.

Her eyes were black rimmed from lack of sleep and worry, and Bill took his thumbs and massaged under her eyes. "This is life, Jane dear," he said softly, "it is life and death. Let's be strong together, and strong in the Lord. He doesn't make any mistakes. He has things all planned out for Pat as He had for you and me."

"Thanks, Mr. Man," she replied, smiling up at him. "I needed that. But my heart just aches for the girl," and her eyes filled with tears.

They walked outside and Bill stood on the steps, looking up at the sky.

"The harmattan winds will come soon," he said, apropos of nothing they had talked about, "and I feel sorry for Pat in that thing."

"Harmattan?" questioned Jane.

"The winds that come before the rains. They are thick with dust, which is picked up on the Sahara Desert and swept along, sometimes so thickly that even the sun is blotted out. The Arabs call it 'the wind of the white horsemen.' We will need someone to work with us each shift when it does come, and perhaps Baru can get some of the men or women to help."

"Biriskilla came the other day to ask if she could help *Mai jinya*," Jane smiled at the memory.

"Good stuff," replied Bill. "You tell Biscuits we need her." Then he headed for the house and a bath.

The harmattan did come, and with it came increasing consciousness and response from Pat. One day she saw Jane looking into her mirror, and with the painful strain that accompanied every word that had to be breathed out with the rhythm of the lung, she said: "Did . . . you . . . tell . . . Mike?"

Jane's response was immediate. "Bill cabled long ago, and he knows by now." The girl's eyes closed contentedly. Jane took a damp towel and wiped her face and lips. She could feel the gritty sand on her own skin. How it must rub the tender skin of the girl so helpless.

She was putting the towel away when she noted the different sound in the room. Alert she looked toward the lung, wondering what it was. Then the awful silence hit her. The power was off!

In panic she went to the door where Biriskilla was sitting on the steps. "Call the *Likita, maza maza,*" she called out, then sped back to the room. Pat was gasping. Remembering the emergency instruction, Jane looked for the handle Bill had pointed out for manual pumping, pulled it loose, and began to count and pump, count and pump, one, two, three . . . one, two, three. How long she had worked at that she didn't know. Her arms ached and sweat was pouring down her face, soaking her dress. She tried to get a look at Pat's face, but could not see clearly. The dreadful gasping had stopped, and whether she was dead or alive, Jane could not tell.

Her sense of relief when she heard pounding steps was almost more than she could bear. Bill burst into the room, with Wigle right behind him. The men took in the situation at a glance. Bill took a compulsive look at the patient, saw the quiet movement of her nostrils and reached over, without missing a beat, and took the handle from Jane.

Wigle stood for a moment, then left the room and headed for the shed where the motor stood, now silent and cold. It was nearly half an hour before he found the trouble. Then sweating and grimy he heard the sweet music of the machine. He grinned behind the dirt that streaked his face.

The same face looked into the lung room a few minutes later. He signalled Bill, who grunted with relief. Holding the manual pump arm, he heard the smooth rhythm as the bellows took up their work. That had been close.

Thirty-one

Day by day and week by week, the time passed with the routine becoming more and more automatic. Pat passed from crisis to crisis, until only time was left to tell the extent of her paralysis.

She grew interested in a lizard that each day would crawl up the netting on the only window that she could see, and she kept score of the flies it managed to get daily. At first she found it hard to remember the score from day to day, but her mind began to clear, her memory returned, and she could recognize what was happening around her, although unable to see a great deal except through her mirror.

Bill often sat with her during his watch, telling her lightly and easily about what had hit her so suddenly and drastically. When she painfully asked questions, he answered them fully, so that step by step she knew what was happening and what might happen.

Once a day one of them would read with her; and each one took time to pray with and for her while sitting beside the lung. Her courage rose higher and higher as the paralysis released something of its deadly hold.

Two months had sped by before Bill felt that he would dare begin some therapy on the girl, and even then he knew that there was scarcely any hope that she might recover any use of her limbs. Then one day he asked her if she was willing to do some work for him, and he grinned down at her. The smile came back via the mirror, and Bill knew her courage was in full bloom.

Carefully he explained what he was going to do, warning her that as soon as she felt she had had enough to let him know. Then with Jane beside him, he undid the clasps that had held her prisoner for so long, and slowly lifted the section.

Pulling the stretcher out slightly, he watched the girl. Released for a moment from the lung, she gasped, and he rapidly pushed it in again. He waited for a moment, then repeated the process. Each time, she could stay out for a fraction longer, and each time there was the exertion to make her lungs work on their own.

It took days before she could stand the pain of being out even for a minute or two, and it was weeks before he could consider anything more drastic than having her breathing without aid.

Once she responded to that, her progress was as quick as she could take it. Slight exercises for muscles that throbbed with pain whenever they were touched came next, with Bill as tender as a nurse in his care of the girl. And week by week the improvements were noticeable.

One of the exercises which she found it hard to erase from her memory afterwards was that of stretching the muscles of her legs while they were still extremely tender to the touch. She would allow the doctor to take one leg at a time, bend the knee sufficiently to straighten it outside the box, bend it and return it to its position. The stretcher had to be pulled out far enough to permit this, or else the leg had to be bent at a much more acute angle with consequent excruciating pain. Sometimes she screamed with pain, walking her fingers painfully up her trunk, across her chest, up her throat and so to her mouth in an attempt to stifle the scream. Bill could only admire the courage of the girl.

When the time came for her to be weaned from the machine which she had grown to loathe, she felt that this was freedom indeed. But five minutes outside and she was begging to be put back in, dropping with relief into her rubber collar.

Five minutes in the morning, five minutes in the evening, and each day adding a fraction of a minute to the time, until finally she could stay out most of a day, but still slept in it at night.

Then Bill decided that she must be free of it completely, and one day, after she had been lying out of it for several hours, he appeared with Merle Wigle.

"This is it, Pat," and he smiled down at her. "No more help with the breathing. From now on you are on your own."

She looked startled for a minute. "You're sure it's safe, Bill?" she asked tremulously. It had saved her life.

"Sure," he said, crossing his heart in mockery. "And Jane or Mrs. Wigle will sit up with you each night until you are sure too."

The men picked up the cot, and raising her gently to waist height, they carried her out of the room. Jane was waiting at the door, and threw a quilt over the girl. Then the three stepped into the sunshine, bearing their burden.

The first look at the outdoors in over two months made Pat squint, until Jane stepped up and shaded her face. Then as she was taken slowly down the steps and along the path, she saw the people lining the way.

"Blessing on you, *Mai jinya*," they called. "God heal you," cried another. And each one looked with love on this wasted white girl who had come to help them and who needed so much help now.

It was blessed relief to sink into the bed, whose cool sheets and soft pillow had been unknown to her for the long weeks in the lung. The relief was too great. Tears rolled down her cheeks, the eyes closed, and the girl fell into a deep sleep.

The daily change was phenomenal. Biriskilla was given charge of the patient so that the others could get their work done, and each one was busy — Bill at the hospital, Jane in the school and visiting in the town, Mrs. Wigle with the whole compound under her thumb, and the quiet spouse beginning to work on the hatchery that he hoped to have built before the heavy rains came. Once more the even tempo of the mission station was felt, the strain of the past months almost gone.

The paralysis still gripped most of Pat's body, but each day she tried something new, encouraged by Bill who felt that his therapy was doing her so much good.

Her first desire was to feed herself. The dish would be placed on her chest, usually with soft bread cut up into small squares in it. Pat would walk her fingers to the dish, and then with a piece of bread imprisoned in her fingers, she would continue this spider like movement to her mouth. Her satisfaction knew no bounds when she had successfully accomplished this feat.

Again she would work until her brow was beaded with perspiration trying to move her leg or wiggle her toes. Biriskilla would hold the part that was being worked on, and would shout triumphantly at any motion, no matter how small. Then she would take a towel and wipe the perspiration from the head of the patient.

And bit by bit, movement came back. The paralysis left her body in the reverse order in which it came, leaving wasted muscle behind.

It was another four months, with the rains finished and the dry season once more coming with its heat, before Bill dared to sit down and plan the future with her. When he thought that she could consider it, he sat down beside her bed.

She looked up at him quizzically, seeing the wrinkles that were beginning to form on his face, the tired look in his eyes.

"I've been a real strain on you, haven't I, Bill?" she asked at last.

He shook his head, smiling down at her. "You are my prize patient," he corrected her, "and I'm proud of what we have done. And thank God for it too," he added, "for I'm convinced now that the Wigles' coming, the arrival of the lung and all the equipment are part of His 'all things work together for good to those that love Him.'"

"'To those who are the called according to His purpose,'" finished Pat. "Bill, I don't know what all this is going to mean, but I have been resting in Him in such peace as I have never known before. I guess my work out here is finished, almost before it is begun," and she sighed, tears in her voice.

"Whoa!" said Bill taking out a handkerchief and wiping her eyes, "don't go soft on me. Not just when I came in to talk to you."

She smiled through the tears. "Sorry. Just let me have a good blow and I'll be all right." She took the handkerchief, and painfully blew her nose. "Now I'm all right," she said, and lay there smiling.

"Okay. Now we talk." He clasped his big hands between his knees in his characteristically boyish gesture. "I have had word from mission headquarters," he began, "and it looks as though we might be able to fly you home, providing you have someone accompany you all the way." He noted the frown on her face. "Now don't go jumping to conclusions," he waved his hand. "Your escort is ready to go with you."

"We sure are, 'dearie," said a voice that made them start slightly. Into the room marched the Wigles, grins on their faces. "We are your escort, and although I don't care for that there flying, anything to help you and we'll do it. Won't we, Merle?" and she looked at her husband.

Bill tried not to grin. This was the impression he had of them on board ship. Yet now it seemed different, and Merle took the cue.

"I find that it will be best if I go back and make some arrangements to come back again and help Bill," he was speaking in that beautifully modulated voice, "and when we heard that we could help you and also get our work done in quick order — well, we're ready to go anytime you are."

Jane had come in behind them, and nodded her approval. And suddenly it swept over Pat. She would be leaving this work, these wonderful people, this country. And she was crying, great rending sobs. Bill turned helplessly to his wife, but it was Mrs. Wigle who was there. "Now, now dearie," the massive hand smoothed the hair back from her brow, "shut up them there tears. Home it is, and in God's good time you will be back on your feet and maybe even here again," and she took the girl's head to her bosom.

It took several days for the arrangements for her safe transportation to the railhead where she would take the short flight to the great airfield at Kano. Bill and Baru rigged up the inside of the Wigles' station wagon until it was as comfortable as her room. The doctor and Mr. Wigle would travel with her, while Jane, Alma, and Baru would ride with the proud Garba in his lorry.

Everything possible was done for the patient, and it was a not too exhausted girl whose stretcher lay on the airfield tarmac, waiting to be lifted into the plane for the first lap of the journey home.

Bill stood by her side. "I have given the Wigles full instructions about you," he was saying, surreptitiously feeling her pulse. "There is a man that I want you to see, or who will see you as soon as you arrive in the city. I don't know what the final outcome will be," he went on, "but I would say from what I have seen of your recovery thus far, that you should get partial recovery of your arms and legs. At the worst you may have to use a wheel chair," he went on, "and at the best crutches. Some patients have almost completely recovered except for a slight limp and excessive tiredness when the walking is not on the level. I cannot prophesy the future, I don't know what it holds — "

"But we know who holds the future, don't we?" interrupted Pat.

Bill looked down at her. "Good girl," he smiled. "With that faith you'll win. God bless you," and he turned to leave.

Jane knelt down on the ground and took the girl's head in her hands. "Be brave, Pat, and we'll be praying for you." A quick kiss and she too turned back.

The Wigles were waving as the men picked up the stretcher. Carrying it as though it was fragile, they hoisted it through the open door of the plane. Pat could only see the Wigles bustling in before her. Then the door clanged, her stretcher was strapped down, and in a few minutes the plane was off. *I'm going home,* rang through Pat's mind, *I'm going home.* Then a face came into her memory, and she wept. It was Mrs. Wigle, ever watchful, who saw the tears. She wiped them away, and for once was silent.

Thirty-two

"Ten minutes and we land at Malton Airport," the voice came over the public address system. "Fasten your seat belts, please. No smoking."

A stewardess came forward to strap the stretcher and patient down, assisted by Mr. Wigle, who with his wife had not left Pat alone for a minute. Indeed, that quiet man, efficient and able, had gone ahead, making arrangements here, clearing the way there, so that Pat's journey home had been swift and uneventful, if inconvenient. Now in ten minutes it would be over.

The plane touched down, gave several slight bumps, then rolled smoothly, with whining tires, on to the runway. Slower and slower, then the brakes took hold, and the great craft swung gently around for its run to its parking slot. The stewardess come forward to loosen the great web belts that held Pat's stretcher rigid and safe.

The airship had stopped now, and the steps were being wheeled into place. First in through the doorway were two white-coated attendants. On instructions from the stewardess, they picked up the stretcher, and with consummate skill, worked it along the narrow aisle, raised it shoulder high to make the sharp turn, and then down the steps, head low, feet high to compensate for the steep steps.

An ambulance was near the plane, and slowly it backed into a better position. Pat's eyes were closed, seeking to overcome her emotion at what might lie before her.

Then a voice, the voice. She would never forget it. She opened her eyes, and kneeling beside her, unashamedly weeping, his face contorted with the pain and agony of love, was Michael Woods.

"Darling," one hand caressed the hair, once so lustrous, now drab and colorless. "Darling," the word was tear-choked as he looked at the sunken cheeks, once so round, the high cheek bones standing out in sharp relief. Only the eyes were the same, and they looked into his.

157

"Michael, Mike . . ." the words trembled. One hand came up, touched the iron gray hair, to be clasped in a hand that reached up fiercely.

"Pat, it's the old firm, Pat and Mike. We'll be in this together, and — " he was interrupted by the ambulance men. Apologetically he looked up, rose to his feet, and then still holding her hand, he stepped into the wide door of the ambulance with her. Wisely, the Wigles gave their orders to the ambulance, then moved to clear their own things and Pat's luggage through customs. They had heard of this teacher who had loved and lost Pat to the service of Christ. Now it seemed as though things would be different after all. They smiled at each other.

In the silence of the ambulance, Mike sat on the jump seat at the side, still holding Pat's hand. Words were unnecessary. It seemed so right for him to be there.

The siren had opened a way for the ambulance, and as it throbbed into silence, Mike bent over the girl.

"Pat?" Her eyes turned to his. In them was the wonderment of love, and he almost forgot to speak. Then, "Remember Peter Dunning's message the night you walked forward, and I came at the last?" She nodded her head. "He spoke of a tangled mountain. You and I will go over this one together," and he didn't dare to speak more.

"Together," she whispered finally, "together with our Armor Bearer." She found strength somewhere to squeeze his hand. The ambulance sped on.